Return to HorrorLand

Look for more books in the Goosebumps Series 2000
by R.L. Stine:

#1 *Cry of the Cat*
#2 *Bride of the Living Dummy*
#3 *Creature Teacher*
#4 *Invasion of the Body Squeezers, Part I*
#5 *Invasion of the Body Squeezers, Part II*
#6 *I Am Your Evil Twin*
#7 *Revenge R Us*
#8 *Fright Camp*
#9 *Are You Terrified Yet?*
#10 *Headless Halloween*
#11 *Attack of the Graveyard Ghouls*
#12 *Brain Juice*

Return
to HorrorLand

AN
APPLE
PAPERBACK

SCHOLASTIC INC.
New York Toronto London Auckland Sydney
Mexico City New Delhi Hong Kong

A PARACHUTE PRESS BOOK

ISBN 0-590-18733-3

Copyright © 1999 by Parachute Press, Inc.
All rights reserved. Published by Scholastic Inc.
APPLE PAPERBACKS, SCHOLASTIC, and associated logos are trademarks and/or registered trademarks of Scholastic Inc.
GOOSEBUMPS is a registered trademark of Parachute Press, Inc.

12 11 10 9 8 7 6 5 4 3 2 1   9/9 0 1 2 3 4/0

Printed in the U.S.A.   40

First Scholastic printing, January 1999

hy did my brother, Luke, and I return to HorrorLand?

We never planned on it. We never wanted to see that terrifying place again. We tried not to think about our narrow escape last summer from that frightening park.

Now, it was a gray winter day six months later. Rain pattered on the den window. Blasts of wind shook the glass.

I gazed at the TV, waiting for my favorite show to begin.

Without any warning, icy fingers gripped my neck.

"*The ghoul attacks!*" a voice rasped.

"Luke — let *go* of me!" I shrieked. I grabbed my brother's wrists and tugged his hands away.

"Ha ha. He got you, Lizzy!" Luke's friend Clay

tossed back his head and giggled. Clay thinks my brother is a riot. He laughs at every obnoxious thing Luke does.

I jumped off the couch, tackled Luke, and pinned him to the floor. "Why are your hands so cold?" I demanded angrily.

Luke grinned up at me. "I put them in the freezer."

Clay thought that was hilarious too. He laughed and slapped the arms of his chair.

Is there anything dumber in the world than a ten-year-old boy?

Yes. *Two* ten-year-old boys.

"Why don't you go put your *head* in the freezer!" I snapped at Luke. Sitting on his chest, I pressed his skinny arms to the floor.

"Get off me, Lizzy," he growled.

"Make me," I replied.

Okay, okay. Hanging out with ten-year-olds makes me a little obnoxious too. I'm supposed to be the calm one in the Morris family. But sometimes Luke sends me over the edge.

"Get off me!" he pleaded. "I . . . can't . . . breathe!"

His face turned bright red. He struggled to squirm free. But he wasn't strong enough to throw me off.

"This is the only way to get you to sit still," I said. Luke has way too much energy. He's always bouncing off the walls. He can't even stay still when he's asleep. He falls out of bed at least once a night. Really!

"Hey — the show is coming on," Clay interrupted. "Cut it out, you two."

I climbed off Luke, tucked my T-shirt back into my jeans, and returned to my place on the couch. I rubbed the back of my neck. It still felt cold from his icy fingers.

Luke stood up, grumbling. He brushed back his straight black hair and dropped onto the arm of Clay's chair. He grinned at me and stuck out his tongue.

Very mature.

I glared back at him. But it's impossible to stay angry at someone who looks so much like you.

Luke and I are both tall and thin. We both have blue eyes, straight black hair, and very fair skin. If I wasn't two years older and four inches taller, we really would look like twins.

"Look out!" he cried. He scraped both hands over Clay's head, messing up his hair.

Clay twisted away. But instead of getting angry, he laughed. I told you — he thinks everything Luke does is hilarious. Clay even thinks it's funny when Luke smears his eyeglasses with his thumbs.

Weird.

Clay is short and stocky. With his glasses, his round face, and his short, feathery blond hair, he reminds me of a chubby owl.

He tried to straighten his hair. But Luke messed

it up again. Then the two of them started a playful shoving match. Clay gave Luke a hard elbow shove. Luke fell off the chair arm and landed hard on the floor.

"Be quiet. It's starting," I scolded.

"It's a strange world . . .," the deep voice on the TV screen announced. "And now it's time to prove it — on *The Strange Report*."

Luke and I love *The Strange Report*. It has the weirdest people in the world, telling the weirdest stories. Derek and Margo Strange are the hosts. They are a husband-and-wife team who travel all over the world, searching for wackos and weirdos.

Last week, they had a man on who ate his own car. He said he could eat anything. He ate a bicycle on camera to prove it. Next he was going to eat a live parrot — but they stopped him in time.

One of my favorites was a woman who owned a hundred cats. She knew them all by name. She said she gave each one of them a tongue bath every day. They showed the woman licking one of her cats. Yuck. It was really gross.

Luke and I laugh our heads off at this show.

"It's *sick*," Clay insists. "It's totally sick."

I guess that's why Luke and I like it so much.

Where do Derek and Margo Strange find these people?

"Look at this kid!" Luke exclaimed, pointing at the screen. "What's he doing on this show? He looks *normal*!"

4

The kid seemed to be about my age. His name appeared on the bottom of the screen: Evan Ross. He was squeezing a ball of gloppy green stuff in one hand.

"It's very dangerous," he was telling Margo Strange. "If people eat a little of it, they'll start to grow."

"What do you call it?" Margo asked the kid.

"Monster Blood," he replied.

Margo nodded solemnly. She has a very pretty, very serious face. With her straight coppery hair, green eyes, and full red lips, she looks a lot like Agent Scully on *The X-Files*.

Margo never laughs at her guests. Even when they are totally nuts. She and Derek always take them seriously.

The camera moved down to a metal bucket on a table beside the kid named Evan. The bucket was filled with Monster Blood. The green goop bubbled over the top.

"And you say that Monster Blood can turn a person into a giant?" Margo asked Evan.

Evan nodded. "Animals too," he said, dropping the blob of green stuff into the bucket. "At school, our classroom hamster ate some, and it turned him into a giant killer hamster!"

Luke and Clay burst out laughing. "Whoa! A giant hamster!" Luke declared. "King Kong Hamster!" He jumped up, strutting and grunting like a gorilla, pounding his chest.

"This kid just wants to get on TV!" Clay snickered. "What a phony baloney."

"We have some videotape," Derek Strange said. "Someone in Evan's school had a camcorder and shot this home video of Cuddles the hamster."

"This I've got to see!" I declared, leaning closer to the TV.

They switched to the videotape. The picture was dark and blurry. I could see a school hallway. A long row of lockers.

Then I heard a roar. It sounded like a lion's roar, very angry. I heard kids screaming. The picture bounced and jerked.

And a huge, furry brown creature rumbled into the hall. It opened its mouth in a ferocious roar. And swung huge brown paws.

"That's Cuddles," Evan explained over the roars and cries of the videotape. "That's Cuddles *after* Monster Blood."

The huge hamster twitched its pink nose. Its whiskers batted against the tile walls.

Luke, Clay, and I fell on the floor laughing.

"That can't be real!" Clay cried. "It's got to be someone in a big hamster costume!"

"It's sick! Sick!" Luke declared, laughing and slapping the floor.

"Why are you kids watching this?" a voice called. All three of us turned to see Mom in the den doorway. She had her arms crossed in front of her. She frowned at the TV screen.

6

"Why do you watch such a dumb show?" she demanded. "What a waste of time."

"But it's *funny*!" I protested. "See this kid with the giant hamster? He has this green stuff —"

I didn't get to finish. The front doorbell chimed.

"I'll get it!" I cried. I pushed past Mom and scrambled to the door.

"Who is it?" I called out.

I pulled the door open. Uttered a startled gasp.

And stared out at Derek and Margo Strange.

2

"**H**uh? Whuh?" I tried to speak, but no words came out.

Derek Strange narrowed his eyes at me. Margo Strange smiled. In person, her red hair was even brighter and her eyes were even greener than on TV.

"Are you Lizzy Morris?" Margo asked.

"Whuh? Uh . . ."

"Who is it?" Mom stepped up behind me. She also let out a gasp as she recognized our two visitors.

"Mrs. Morris?" Margo asked, a smile spreading over her dark red lips.

"The kids were just watching you on TV!" Mom exclaimed.

"M-Monster Blood," I choked out, my heart pounding.

"Oh, right. The Monster Blood show," Derek

said, chuckling. "We taped that show in Atlanta a few weeks ago."

"What a weird kid," Margo said. "He swore his story was true. But Derek and I didn't really believe it." She wiped a splash of rainwater off her forehead.

"Come in. Come in," Mom said, holding open the storm door. "It's still raining. You're getting all wet."

I saw a long white limousine parked at the foot of our driveway. "I can't believe you're really here!" I gushed, starting to feel a little more normal.

"We flew in from New York to see you," Margo said. "It's great to be back in Chicago again."

Mom led them into the den. "We have visitors," she told the boys.

When they saw the Stranges, Luke and Clay nearly exploded. Their faces turned bright red. Their mouths burst open. They looked like two balloons about to pop.

"I'm glad you enjoy our show," Margo said, glancing at the TV screen.

"Yes. We came from New York to personally thank you for watching!" Derek said. He laughed heartily to show he was joking.

I stared at him. How was this possible? Derek Strange standing in *my* den? He was tall and handsome. In person, he looked bigger than on TV. With his straight black mustache and wavy, dark hair, he looked a little like Tom Selleck.

Except I saw now that his hair wasn't real. The

9

top didn't match the sides. Standing this close, I could see the line of his toupee. It looked as if he were wearing a furry black cat on his head!

"We came to talk to you about something very important," Margo said.

"Sit down. Sit down, please!" Mom twittered. "What can I bring you? Would you like some coffee?"

Margo shivered and hugged herself. "Coffee would be nice. I got a little chilled in the rain."

She straightened the sleeves of her navy blue business suit and then perched on the edge of the couch. Derek dropped down heavily beside her, loosening his tie.

"I'll be right back with the coffee," Mom said. "Then we can talk about why you've come." She hurried to the kitchen.

Luke clicked off the TV. "I'm Luke and this is my friend Clay," he said.

"We know," Derek Strange replied.

I held my breath. What a weird thing to say, I thought. Why does he know us? Why have they come here?

"What are you doing here?" Luke blurted out.

Derek leaned forward, still tugging at his tie. His dark eyes moved from Luke to Clay to me. "Some evil aliens landed in your backyard," he said softly. "They plan to kidnap the three of you in their spacecraft and operate on you. Margo and I are going to film it."

3

"Excuse me?" My mouth dropped open.

Derek burst out laughing.

Margo gave him a playful shove. "Shut up, Derek," she scolded, shaking her head. She turned back to us. "Don't pay any attention to him. He has a sick sense of humor."

"I must have a sick sense of humor," Derek told her, grinning. "I married *you*!" He laughed at his own joke.

I couldn't take my eyes off the furry toupee perched on Derek's head. He looked so young and handsome on TV. Up close, he appeared much older, with yellow skin and wrinkles under his eyes. I tried to picture him bald.

Margo's voice broke into my thoughts. "I understand you've been to HorrorLand," she said, her green eyes locking on mine.

"It was . . . scary," Clay muttered.

"It was *gross*!" Luke cried. "Our car blew up and the monsters turned out to be real and —"

"How did you know we were there?" I interrupted him. "That was last summer."

"We saw the HorrorLand attendance records," Derek replied. "Actually, we stole them from the park. And we found your names and addresses on the list."

"We want to do a show about HorrorLand," Margo added, lowering her voice to a whisper. "Derek and I want to take you back to Horror-Land and film you."

"No way!" Luke and I cried in unison.

"I'm never going back there!" Clay exclaimed, shaking his head.

"What's going on?" Mom asked cheerily. She returned to the den, carrying a tray with the coffeepot and mugs. "Have we found out the reason for this mysterious visit?"

"They want to take us to HorrorLand!" Luke blurted out.

Mom's face tightened into a fretful frown as she set the tray down on the coffee table. She shuddered. "That dreadful, frightening place," she murmured. "Why would anyone want to go there?"

"We think something suspicious is going on

there," Margo replied. "Maybe something very dangerous."

"We think the TV viewers should be warned about HorrorLand," Derek added, reaching for the coffeepot and pouring himself a mug. "We want to find out why the park keeps moving every few months. Did you know it moved to Florida a few weeks ago?"

"No. We didn't," Mom said, shaking her head.

"We want to expose HorrorLand," Derek continued. "Maybe put it out of business."

"But why do you want to take *us* there?" I demanded, my voice shaking.

"You've been there," Derek replied. "You know what to expect."

"But — but —" I stammered. "Isn't it just some kind of cable TV horror show with monsters? Last summer, they told us it was all just a game show."

"We don't think so," Margo replied solemnly. "We want to find out the truth. We —"

"I'm very sorry," Mom interrupted, frowning. "But it's much too terrifying. I'm afraid you two people have traveled a long way for nothing. I can't allow the children to return to that park."

Margo set down her coffee mug. "But they'll be perfectly safe," she told Mom. "Derek and I will never let them out of our sight. We'll be right there, taping them secretly, taping everything that happens. The kids will never be in any real danger."

Mom bit her bottom lip. "I don't think so," she replied thoughtfully.

"And we are prepared to pay you ten thousand dollars," Derek said. "For one weekend."

I saw Mom swallow hard. Her expression softened.

We could really use ten thousand dollars. Dad lost his job at the bank. He has been working only part-time since the fall.

Mom sighed. "Well . . . maybe if my husband and I came along."

"I'm sorry," Margo said. "We can't take you. Derek and I have to pretend to be the parents."

Mom thought some more. "You're sure the kids will be perfectly safe?" she asked.

"Perfectly safe," Derek replied, raising his right hand as if swearing an oath. "Margo and I will be right there with them, taping what goes on. I promise you they'll be okay, Mrs. Morris."

"Well . . ." Mom hesitated. "I have to check with my husband. Let me go call him."

Luke and I exchanged glances. It appeared that we were about to return to HorrorLand. How did we feel about that? Horrified? Excited? Sick?

I couldn't decide.

"Can Clay come too?" Luke asked the Stranges. "He was with us last summer."

Margo nodded. "Yes — if his parents approve."

"Do we . . . do we have to go on the rides?" Clay

stammered. His eyes were wide behind his glasses. He had that frightened owl look again.

"Remember that floating coffin ride?" Luke asked him. "And the Doom Slide?"

"Yuck." Clay made a sick face.

"We want to show the world how horrifying that park is," Margo said. "We want to show everyone how dangerous it is. How irresponsible the owners are."

"But do we have to go on *everything*?" Clay asked in a tiny voice.

Mom returned before the Stranges could answer. She nodded solemnly. "It's okay with us," she told them, "as long as you guarantee their safety."

"We guarantee it," Derek said with a smile. "Thank you for cooperating."

Margo was applying a fresh coat of red lipstick to her lips. "We'll come back for you next Friday," she said. "And we'll all fly down to Florida together. We can talk about our plans on the plane."

"We'll bring you the check for ten thousand dollars next Friday," Derek promised Mom, climbing to his feet. He turned to us kids. "You're not really frightened — are you?"

"Uh . . . well . . ." I hesitated.

"No way," Luke said. He always has to be the brave one. "I'm not scared. I can't wait."

Clay didn't say a word.

"It would be exciting to be on TV," I said.

"Yeah. That would be totally cool," Luke agreed.

"You won't regret this," Derek said, pulling his overcoat around him as he headed to the front door.

We said good-bye. Clay promised to get a permission letter from his parents. Mom closed the door after them.

I stepped up to the front window and watched the Stranges hurry down the driveway to their limo.

I can't believe this is happening, I told myself. I can't believe we're going back to HorrorLand. What a shock.

And then, peering out the window, I got another shock.

As Derek Strange turned to open the limo door, I saw a fat green tail poke out from under his coat.

hen Derek and Margo came to pick us up on Friday, I didn't waste any time. As soon as Luke, Clay, and I climbed into their van, I turned to Derek. "Last week, I watched from the window when you left," I told him. "And when you turned around, I saw a green tail."

He laughed.

Margo's eyes went wide. Then she laughed too.

"It was a joke," Derek explained. "I forgot it was still there."

"The tail was sewn onto the back of his coat," Margo said. "Derek was supposed to wear white tie and tails for a very fancy party we were filming."

"So I thought it would be funny to wear a *real* tail," Derek continued. "We flew out to see you so quickly, I didn't have time to remove it."

Margo's expression turned serious. "I hope it didn't upset you. It was just a joke."

"Just because our name is Strange doesn't mean we really are strange!" Derek exclaimed. He laughed again.

As we rode to the airport, I began to feel a lot better. Derek and Margo were so nice. I couldn't believe I was riding in a car with real TV stars!

I could tell that Luke was excited too. He didn't get into any shoving matches with Clay or bounce up and down in the seat or sing off-key at the top of his lungs. He was acting fairly human — for him. I guessed he was trying to impress the Stranges.

Clay barely said a word. He stared out the car window, his round face tight with worry.

Clay was terrified the *first* time, I remembered. Why did he agree to return? He probably wants to be on TV, I figured. Just like Luke and me.

Freezing rain spattered the windshield. Derek clicked the wipers to high speed.

"At least you guys will be escaping winter for a while," Margo said. The limo pulled up to the airport terminal.

An hour later, we were seated in first class, on our way to HorrorLand. Derek and Margo explained their plan to us. "We're going to dress up like typical tourists," Derek said. "You know. T-shirts and baggy shorts. Camcorder strapped around my neck. We're going to be a family on vacation, enjoying the park."

"Except we'll be taping the frightening things they do to people at HorrorLand," Margo added. She sighed, sweeping a strand of red hair off her forehead. "We haven't been able to find out who owns the park. Or who runs it. Or why they try to terrify kids."

"But we will," Derek promised. "With your help, we'll find out the truth about HorrorLand." He grinned. "And . . . we'll get a great TV show out of it."

"And we'll be TV stars when we come back!" Luke declared, pumping a fist in the air.

Derek's face twisted in surprise. "Come back?" he asked. "When you come back?" He stared hard at Luke. "Don't you think it might make a more dramatic show if you three don't survive?"

All three of us stared at Derek.

"Don't survive?" I gasped.

"But you promised our parents!" Clay whined.

Derek burst out laughing.

"You're not funny," Margo groaned. "Stop making jokes, Derek. You have a sick sense of humor. You really do."

The huge billboard rose up like a monster in front of our rented minivan. I gasped as the two gigantic yellow eyes stared down at me.

Derek slowed the van, and we squinted through the Saturday morning sunlight at the billboard. The monster on the billboard was a painting of a HorrorLand Horror. It appeared to reach out of the sign.

"The park workers are called Horrors, right?" Margo asked.

"Yes. And they're real monsters!" Luke cried.

"Are you sure?" Derek asked. "Aren't they just people wearing costumes?"

"Trust me," Luke said firmly. "Real monsters."

Margo scribbled something on a little pad. "Well, that's one of the first things we'll check out. Are the park workers human or monster?"

I shivered, thinking about the Horrors. They had green skin, bulging yellow eyes, and dark horns curling over their heads. They had pointed green tails at the back of their costumes. And they all spoke in dry, raspy voices and tried to be scary.

The five of us stared out the van window at the painted Horror above the billboard. "This . . . this brings back a lot of bad memories," Clay whispered.

Clay was right. Just seeing that evil, grinning monster face made me want to turn around and forget the whole thing.

"It's *so cool!*" Luke gushed. He read the billboard words out loud: "Welcome to HorrorLand, where nightmares come to life!"

"The painting is so real," Clay murmured, pressing himself as far back in the seat as he could.

Derek drove a little further along the narrow country road. All I could see were flat, empty farm fields on all sides. But soon, the shadow of another big billboard washed over us.

THE HORRORLAND HORRORS WELCOME YOU TO HORRORLAND.

And then a smaller sign beside it:

UNDER NEW MISMANAGEMENT.

"We're getting close," Derek called back to us. "Are you kids getting excited?"

"Yes!" Luke cried. He was the only one to answer.

"Check the camcorder," Derek instructed Margo. "Make sure we have plenty of tape cassettes."

"I checked it three times," Margo grumbled. But she obediently opened the camcorder case and counted the cassettes.

"We're here! Here's the parking lot," Derek declared. He turned sharply. We pulled past a black-and-yellow traffic sign: CAUTION — KIDS SCREAMING.

"It's not very crowded," Margo said. "Only twenty or thirty cars."

Derek pulled into a parking space at the end of the first row. I took a deep breath and followed the boys out of the van.

A tall black metal fence stretched the width of the park. Behind the fence, I could see dark buildings, tall towers, food carts, people standing in line. The mournful sound of organ music floated through the fence.

I saw an open gate next to a small ticket booth. A sign above the gate read:

ENTRANCE ONLY. NO ONE EVER EXITS.

22

"Well?" Derek grinned at us. "Do we look like tourists? Do we look like a family on vacation?"

I turned and stared at them. They both were disguised as normal tourists.

Derek had a stubble of black beard on his face. He wore a loose green T-shirt, pulled down over baggy red-and-blue plaid shorts.

On his feet, Derek had brown leather sandals over black kneesocks. And he had turned an aqua-and-white Florida Marlins cap sideways on his head.

He looked like a total geek.

Margo's outfit was just as bad. A shiny gold tank top and black spandex bike shorts. Bright red sneakers with orange laces. The sneakers matched the giant red plastic, heart-shaped sunglasses that covered her eyes and half her face.

She had a fake tattoo of a Cupid surrounded by red and blue flowers on one arm just below the shoulder.

"I like this look," she declared, laughing. "I might just keep it!"

Clay studied them. "But what if they recognize you?" he asked.

We all burst out laughing. There was *no way* anyone would ever guess these were two of the most famous TV stars in the country!

Derek raised the camcorder in one hand. "Let's get started," he said, turning serious. "We've got a program to do."

He led the way to the ticket booth. My heart started to pound as we walked closer to the park. My hands were suddenly ice-cold.

The chilling organ music swirled around us. In the far distance, I could hear shrill screams.

As we stepped up to the ticket booth, a green-skinned Horror leaned out and smiled at us. "Welcome to HorrorLand," she rasped.

"This looks like fun!" Derek exclaimed. "Right, kids?"

"Right!" the three of us echoed brightly.

Margo tugged Derek's sleeve. "Honey, are you sure this park is safe?" she asked.

"Yes, it's perfectly safe," the Horror replied. "Safe for us Horrors!" She uttered a hoarse laugh. As she leaned over, her curled horns tapped the bars of the ticket booth.

We all laughed too. But I didn't really feel like laughing.

This park *isn't* safe, I told myself. That's why we're here.

Derek paid for five tickets, and we walked through the gate.

"I can't believe we're back here!" Luke exclaimed. He threw his hands up excitedly and jumped up and down.

He's actually happy to be back, I thought. What a weirdo!

I gazed around. Paths led in all directions. Low,

dark buildings lined the paths. Two Horrors walked by, humming a song together.

My eyes stopped at a large map of the park. A sign above it read: IF YOU NEED THIS MAP, YOU'RE ALREADY LOST.

"Let's check out the map," I said. I took a few steps toward it — then stopped as a tall, fierce-looking Horror moved quickly to block our path.

"Ha ha. Great costume!" Derek said, grinning at the big creature.

The Horror didn't grin back. He narrowed his eyes at Derek's camcorder. "What's that?" he growled.

Derek raised the camcorder. "Just a video camera," Derek replied. "See? We want to remember everything about this vacation — right, kids?"

"Right!" the three of us echoed.

The Horror uttered another angry growl. "Sorry," he rasped. "No cameras."

He grabbed the camcorder from Derek's hand, dropped it to the pavement — and smashed it under his big green foot.

"**H**ave a scary day," the Horror rasped. He turned and stomped away.

I swallowed hard. My mouth suddenly felt very dry, and my heart pounded.

We all stared down at the flattened camcorder.

"Now what?" I muttered.

"We . . . we came all this way for *nothing*!" Clay whined.

Derek waited until the Horror turned a corner and disappeared behind a dark building. "No problem," he said finally.

He reached into a pocket of his baggy plaid shorts and pulled out a tiny silvery camera. "I expected that," Derek said. "That's why I brought the Mini-Super-Eight."

I studied the camera. It fit in the palm of Derek's hand.

"I have one too," Margo said, pulling a tiny camcorder from her bag. "Let's get to work."

"Let's try to cover the park," Derek instructed. "Do as much as we can, and get it on tape. Pick a path, kids, and we'll —"

"I'm kind of hungry," Luke interrupted. "I was too excited to eat breakfast."

"There's a food stand over there," I said, pointing. A Horror in a purple apron leaned against a small cart.

We hurried over to it. The Horror stood up straight and brushed off her apron as we approached. A sign on top of the cart read: FINGERS.

"Great! You've got chicken fingers?" Luke asked her.

She shook her head. "No. Just fingers."

I lowered my eyes to the cart. Steam rose up. I saw piles of fingers toasting inside. *Human* fingers. "Ohhh, gross," I murmured, covering my mouth with a hand.

"They're pretty good with a lot of ketchup," the Horror rasped.

"Uhh . . . no, thanks," Luke choked out.

"I have toes too," the Horror said. "But they're not hot yet."

We hurried away. "I got it on tape," Derek said, patting his tiny camcorder. The sun beamed down.

He turned his Marlins cap around to protect his eyes.

"Those weren't real fingers," Clay said softly. "Were they?"

"It has to be a joke," I told him. The poor guy looked terrified already. And we had only just arrived.

We followed a curving path through rows of tall hedges. I could hear kids' voices on the other side of the hedges.

Luke ran ahead of everyone.

"The park has changed a lot," I commented. "What happened to all the No Pinching signs? They used to be everywhere. Remember? That's how we defeated the Horrors. By pinching them. But now the signs are gone."

"I guess that means it's okay to pinch!" Luke exclaimed. He grabbed Clay and gave his arm a hard pinch. "The Mad Pincher strikes again!"

"Don't start that again, Luke!" I begged.

But the boys ignored me. Clay pinched Luke back. So Luke pinched Clay's cheek until he screamed.

"Check out this pyramid," Margo said. "It looks so old and real."

We stood in the shadow of a tall, pyramid-shaped building, built of pale orange stone. A stern-faced statue of an Egyptian soldier guarded the narrow entrance.

"Mummy Walk!" Luke read the carved words over the entrance.

We followed him up to the open doorway. A stale odor floated out on a blast of cold, damp air.

"Should we try it?" Derek asked.

"It . . . it looks kind of dark in there," Clay murmured, hanging back behind the rest of us.

"It looks totally cool!" Luke declared.

"Let's do it," Margo said, pulling out her camcorder. "Now, remember, guys — stick close together. Derek and I will be taping. We won't be able to see you if you wander off."

"And act natural," Derek added. "Forget about the camera, okay? Just pretend that Margo and I aren't here."

Luke led the way.

I read the sign one more time: MUMMY WALK. Then I took a deep breath and stepped through the narrow doorway, into the darkness.

We were making our first big mistake.

ur footsteps on the stone floor echoed off the walls. "Hellllooooo!" Luke called. And his voice boomed all around us.

"Is anybody in here?" I called. My voice came out high and tiny, but it echoed around the vast chamber.

I waited for my eyes to adjust to the darkness. Blinking, I saw that the high walls were covered with ancient-looking drawings. Cats and other animal faces. Flat-looking people all turned sideways.

We followed the walkway into a narrow hallway. It opened into another dark chamber. The air grew colder. A stale odor followed us.

"This is creepy," Clay whispered.

"Where are the mummies?" Luke demanded. "There are supposed to be mummies — right?"

Our sneakers squeaked over the stone floor as we headed toward a dim orange light across the chamber.

A loud *HISSSS* made me stop. I grabbed Luke's arm. "What was that?"

"Ohhhh." A low moan escaped Clay's throat. The orange light reflected in his glasses. Behind it, I could see his eyes bulge in fright.

Another *HISSSS*.

I squinted into the light, a dim triangle of orange from the ceiling spreading over the floor.

"Whoa." The floor under the light appeared to be moving. Wriggling.

No.

Not the floor.

As I squinted, the snakes came into focus.

At first, I saw three heads hissing, snapping, curling over each other. Oh, wow! It's a three-headed snake, I thought.

A huge, three-headed snake.

I froze, still gripping my brother's arm.

And realized I was staring at *three* snakes. Rolling over each other, curling and uncurling, hissing loudly, their slender tongues darting from their open mouths.

"Th-they're not real," Clay stammered, backing up.

Two more snake heads raised up from the floor. Shiny black eyes gleamed at us across the dark room.

They snapped at each other, hissing loudly.

Two more snakes uncurled from the pile.

A snake pit, I realized. I'd only read about them in books. And now I was staring at dozens of snakes — so long and thick — all tangled around each other. Pulling and twisting. Snapping their jaws. And hissing . . . hissing . . .

I covered my ears against the frightening, shrill sound.

"Let's get out of here!" I cried.

"No. This is cool!" Luke declared.

He broke free of my grip and moved quickly toward the hissing, snapping snakes.

"Luke — *stop!*" I shrieked.

He spun around and laughed at me. "Lizzy — I dare you to come closer!"

"No! No way!" I protested.

He backed up, moving closer to the writhing snakes. "Dare you, Lizzy! Come on! Dare you to come this close!"

"Luke!"

It happened too fast. Too fast to move. Too fast to warn him. Too fast to scream.

I froze — froze in breathless horror — as a snake shot out of the pile — thrust its head forward — and snapped its jaws deep into my brother's leg.

8

"Nooooooo!" The scream finally burst from my throat.

The snake slithered up Luke's back. Its head bobbed over Luke's shoulder.

Bobbed . . . The eyes glowing . . .

It *missed*! I realized.

It snapped — and missed his leg!

Luke didn't react for the longest time. He stood there, staring at me, a sick grin frozen on his face.

His eyes turned toward the snake. He stared at the triangular head, bobbing over his shoulder.

And then Luke lurched forward, scrambling, his arms thrashing, his eyes wild. His shrill scream echoed off the low ceiling.

"They're real!" he shrieked. "I — I didn't know. I didn't think! Th-they're real!"

"Are you okay?" I cried. I checked his leg to make sure the snake hadn't bitten him after all.

His jeans weren't punctured. But poor Luke. His whole body was trembling.

"Real," he murmured. "I thought . . ." He bent down, struggling to calm down and catch his breath.

I turned to the Stranges. "Did you get that on tape?"

Derek shook his head. "Too dark," he muttered. "Too dark in here for these lenses." He frowned at the camcorder. "We need more light."

"Let's find the mummies," Margo said softly, glancing nervously at the snakes. "Those snakes must be puppets or something. They wouldn't have live snakes loose like that in here, would they?"

No one answered. We were too eager to get out of that room and away from the seething snake pit.

But where was the door?

I spun around. And spun around again.

Which way did we come in?

Away from the triangle of orange light, we moved through solid blackness.

And found ourselves in a room we hadn't walked through. A long, low-ceilinged room.

My heart thudding, I stopped to catch my breath. The air felt heavy and damp. The sour smell of mildew, of decay, followed us.

"Real snakes?" Margo murmured. "Were they real or not?" She had taken off the heart-shaped sunglasses. I caught the fear in her eyes.

Derek placed a comforting hand on her shoulder. "They may have been robots. Or maybe computerized puppets. Too dark in there to really tell. Come on, guys. Let's not stop here. Let's keep moving."

"Yeah. Let's find the mummies!" Luke declared, sounding normal again.

We found them in the next room.

As soon as we entered the long, dark room, we saw the two rows of stone mummy cases standing against the walls.

"Yes!" Luke cried happily. "I'll bet *they're* real too. Real mummies!" He took off, heading to the nearest case.

He stopped short a few feet away and uttered a disappointed groan.

"What's wrong?" I called, hurrying up to him.

"It's closed up," he moaned. "Look. The mummy cases. The lids are all closed."

I gazed down the long row of mummy cases. Yes. Luke was right. The cases all had stone lids, shut tight.

"What a rip-off!" Luke complained. "How are you supposed to see the mummies if the lids are all closed?"

He tore off down the row, examining case after case. Clay kept close to him, shaking his head.

I followed behind, walking slowly, my eyes running over the heavy stone cases, wondering if they were empty. Or if real mummies from ancient Egypt stood inside them.

The boys had trotted nearly to the end of the room. "Hey, Luke? Clay? Wait up!" I called.

I stopped with a gasp when I heard the voice.

At first, I thought I was hearing the hiss of a snake.

But then I realized it was a hoarse, whispered voice.

"Let me out. Please — let me out!"

A voice spoke from inside an ancient mummy case.

I stared at the tall stone case. The hoarse, whispered plea rang in my ear.

Silence now.

Had I imagined it? Was Luke playing a joke on me?

No. Luke and Clay were at the other end of the room, examining the lid of a mummy case near the door.

And the hoarse plea repeated itself: "Please — let me out! Let me out!" So soft. The words muffled by the heavy stone lid.

I grabbed the edge of the lid. The stone felt rough and scratchy. "Th-there's someone in here!" I cried.

I tried to pry open the lid.

And then I heard the plea of another hoarse

voice from the next ancient coffin: "Let me out. . . . I have to get out . . ."

And more whispered words from the next coffin: "Help me. Somebody. Help me."

And then voices from all the mummy cases:

"I've been in here so long. . . ."

"Please let me out. . . . Please . . ."

"I'm still alive. . . . Open the lid. . . . I'm still alive. . . ."

Voices all around. I raised my hands to my face. I tugged at the sides of my hair.

And then I realized what I was hearing.

Recorded voices. Taped voices from speakers hidden in the cases. Repeating . . . repeating . . .

"Let me out. . . . Please . . ."

"Let me out. . . ."

Of *course* the voices were recorded. There couldn't be anyone locked in these old cases. No way.

"Hey, Luke!" I turned away and shouted over the hoarse, repeating voices.

"Luke?"

He was gone. Clay too. And I couldn't see the Stranges anywhere.

"Hey — we were supposed to stick together!" I shouted. "Where did you go?"

I took off, my sneakers slapping the stone floor, kicking up thick dust as I ran.

Through the doorway at the end of the long room.

"Luke? Clay?"

I found them in the next room, huddled around a large mummy case, this one not standing up — lying on its back.

"Hey, guys," I scolded, struggling to catch my breath. "Don't run off — okay?"

"Check it out," Luke said, ignoring me. He pointed at the stone lid that tilted straight up over the mummy case. "This one is open," he said.

"But it's empty," Clay added. He stood on tiptoe to peer down into the case.

Luke grinned at me. "Lizzy, I dare you to climb inside," he said.

"No way!" I snapped. "I mean it. No more stupid dares, Luke. The last time you dared me to do something, a snake almost bit your leg off."

Luke's grin didn't fade. His eyes flashed excitedly in the dim chamber light. "Dare you, Lizzy," he repeated. "Dare you to climb inside."

I crossed my arms in front of me. "No way. It's probably filthy in there. And I'll bet it's crawling with all kinds of bugs."

"Dare you," Luke repeated. "Come on, Lizzy. Don't you want to know what it felt like to be a mummy in ancient Egypt? Don't you want to know what it feels like to lie on the bottom of a mummy case?"

"No, I don't," I insisted. "And neither do you."

"Yes, I do!" Luke replied.

Before I could stop him, he gripped the side of

the mummy case with both hands, swung his body up into the air — and dropped inside.

"Luke — *no!*" I screamed.

He giggled and slid down, stretching out on the floor of the mummy case.

"Get out, Luke!" I shouted angrily.

"Get out!" Clay repeated. "Come on. Let's go."

"Out! Come on — out!" I peered over the side of the case at him.

Luke giggled again. Lying on his back, he crossed his arms over his chest, as if he were a real mummy. "This is cool," he murmured.

I jumped back when I heard the creaking sound.

Soft at first. Then louder . . . louder.

And then I screamed as the heavy stone lid came crashing down.

10

The lid landed with a heavy *THUD*. Stone crashed against stone. A wave of dust blew off the case.

Choking, I covered my eyes with my arm. When I lowered it, I saw that the mummy case was shut tight.

"Luke!" I shouted. "Are you okay? Can you hear me?"

No reply.

"Clay — quick! Help me lift the lid!" I choked out.

He and I dove forward. We pressed our hands against the thick stone lid — and pushed up.

"Harder —" I gasped.

I straightened my legs. Tensed my arms. Gritted my teeth.

And *pushed*.

"It won't budge!" Clay wailed.

"Together!" I cried. "Push together. On three. We can do it!"

We leaned forward, pushing against the lid. I counted off. "One — two — *three*!"

We strained, groaning loudly.

No. No go.

"It's too heavy," Clay gasped. "It weighs a ton."

We both fell back, breathing hard. My arms ached. My head throbbed.

I pressed my face against the side of the mummy case. "Luke — can you hear me?" I called in.

I heard a tap on the side of the case. And then two more taps.

"He's okay," I told Clay. "But there can't be much air in there. We've got to get him out — right away!"

I spun around. "Derek! Margo!" I cried.

In all the excitement, I forgot about the Stranges.

"Help us!" I called. "Derek? Margo?"

I squinted all around the dark room.

"Where are you?" I shouted, my voice rising, unable to hide my growing panic. "Help us!"

"They're . . . gone," Clay murmured.

I turned to him. His chin trembled. His round, chubby body shook. He suddenly looked about five years old.

"Where did they go?" he whispered. "They said they would watch us. Protect us."

I turned around and called their names again.

No reply.

"Maybe they saw the lid go down, and they ran to get help," I suggested. "Maybe —"

I stopped when I heard three taps from inside the mummy case. Softer this time. Weaker.

"We can't just stand here," I told Clay. "I've got to get help."

"I'll go with you," he said, his voice trembling.

"No. Wait here," I instructed. "In case somebody comes. In case the Stranges return."

Clay swallowed hard. He cupped his hands around his mouth. And shouted shrilly, "Is anyone in here? Can't anyone hear us?"

No reply.

The echo of Clay's words faded slowly.

"Isn't anyone running this place?" Clay called. "Can't anyone help us?"

Silence.

"Luke is going to suffocate in there," I said. "I've got to hurry."

My legs trembled as I ran through the doorway. My heart thudded in my chest.

"Calm, Lizzy," I murmured out loud. "You're the calm one in the family — remember? You'll get Luke out. He'll be fine."

I ran through a long, dark tunnel. It curved and

43

twisted — until I saw bright light at the end. Sunlight? An exit?

Yes!

I burst out into bright daylight. "Help me! Somebody — help me!" I shouted.

Three Horrors were huddled around a food cart across the path. Two guys, one tall, one very short, and a girl, all wearing purple Horror-Land uniforms. They turned at the sound of my cries.

"Are you lost?" the tallest one asked. "Don't worry. *Everyone* is lost in this park!"

"No —" I cried breathlessly. I didn't want to touch him. So I grabbed the sleeve of his purple uniform. "You've got to come. Hurry!" I dragged him a few steps toward the pyramid.

"What's wrong? Lost your mummy?" the girl Horror joked. Her smile faded when she saw the panic on my face.

"It's my brother —" I choked out. "He climbed into an open mummy case, and the lid slammed down on him. He — he's going to suffocate!"

The Horrors exchanged surprised glances. "An open case?" the girl asked. "There aren't any open cases. They're all closed tight."

They shook their heads, their purple horns glowing in the bright sunlight.

"*Listen to me!*" I shrieked, pulling the tall Horror by the sleeve. "He's trapped in a case! He can't breathe! You've *got* to come!"

He glanced at his green-and-purple wristwatch. "We can't. We're on our break."

"But — it's an *emergency*!" I shrieked.

"We get a twenty-minute break every morning," the girl Horror said calmly. "Then we're back on duty till lunchtime."

"But my brother — he can't breathe in there!" I cried.

"We should probably put up a sign telling people to stay out of the mummy cases," the tall Horror told the other two. "Maybe I'll bring it up at the next meeting."

"But — but —" I sputtered. "Listen to me!"

"I think there are some chains and other equipment over there," the girl Horror said, pointing. "It might help you pull open the case."

I swallowed hard, staring at them in disbelief. They really weren't going to help me.

"Okay," I choked out. I spun away and ran frantically toward the equipment.

"Good luck!" one of them called after me.

I found a pile of chains and pulleys in a small, open closet. I grabbed as much as I could carry. Then, running full speed, I burst back into the tunnel and hurried up to the mummy case in the middle of the room.

Clay slumped beside the case, hands deep in the pockets of his shorts, shaking his head. "Luke hasn't pounded on the side for a long time," he said in a whisper.

I dropped the chains on the floor. Then I leaned over the case and shouted. "Luke — can you hear me? Luke? Are you okay?"

No reply.

"Help me with this stuff!" I barked at Clay.

We picked up the chains and started to pull them over the stone lid. "Where are the Stranges?" Clay asked in a tiny voice. "Where *are* they?"

I shrugged. I didn't know the answer. I pounded on the side of the case with both fists. "Be okay, Luke," I prayed softly. "Please, be okay."

We slid the chains around the lid. Then we wrapped the chain around the pulley. I wasn't sure we were doing it right. But we had to do *something*.

It took only a few minutes. But it seemed like hours to me.

"Okay — pull!" I cried. Clay tugged at the chain while I turned the wheel. The chain clanked as it tightened over the stone lid.

"Come on . . . come *on*!" I muttered through gritted teeth. Clay pulled with all his strength. I spun the pulley, like turning the reel of a fishing rod.

The chains creaked and strained.

Slowly . . . slowly the lid began to slide off.

"Yes! It's working!" I cried happily.

The stone lid ground heavily over the case as it moved, an inch, another inch, another . . .

"Luke!" I cried. "We're getting you out! Luke?"

The chains clanked. The lid slid open.

I dove forward, my heart thudding, and peered into the mummy case. "Luke?"

The case was empty.

A choked cry escaped my open mouth.

"What's wrong?" Clay called in a tiny voice. "Is he . . . okay?"

"He's *gone*!" I gasped.

I leaned over the side of the mummy case, staring at the stone floor. Empty. Empty . . .

I tried to speak, but panic tightened my throat. "Where is my brother?" I finally choked out. "Where is he?"

"We've got to find the Stranges," Clay said in a whisper. "They've got to help us. We have to find the park manager. Maybe the manager will help us."

"Come on. Let's go," I said. I grabbed Clay's hand. It felt cold and wet. I tugged him to the tunnel.

My stomach did flip-flops as we trotted toward the exit. I felt really sick and upset. But I tried to ignore it.

Clay and I burst back out into the sunlight. I glanced around the outside of the pyramid. I saw two kids and their parents entering at the front.

No sign of the three Horrors. The food stand across the path stood empty and deserted.

"Let's try to find the main office," I said, shielding my eyes from the bright sun with one hand.

"Which way?" Clay asked.

"It's probably near the front of the park," I replied.

"But which way is the front?" he whined. The poor guy was really terrified.

So was I. But I kept reminding myself that someone had to stay calm. Someone had to take charge. If only the waves would stop crashing inside my stomach!

"Uh . . . let's go to the pyramid entrance," I suggested, glancing all around. "Maybe we can retrace our steps."

Clay nodded. He followed me as I led the way to the front of the Mummy Walk pyramid.

We turned the corner. Took a few steps.

And then I let out a shriek of surprise.

12

"**L**uke!" I screamed.

"Huh?" Clay gasped. His mouth practically dropped down to his knees.

"Where *were* you?" Luke cried, running up to us.

"Where were *we*?" I shrieked. "Where were *you*?"

"I — I'm not sure," he stammered. "A trapdoor opened in the bottom of the mummy case. I slid down through a long, dark tunnel. I thought I was going to slide forever. And then . . . it dropped me right outside the pyramid."

He squinted at me. "What took you so long to come out?"

"AAAGGGH!" I let out an angry roar. I wrapped my hands around his throat.

I wanted to strangle him. And I wanted to hug him at the same time.

He shoved my hands away. "What's your problem, Lizzy?"

"You — you — you!" I shrieked.

"We were kind of worried," Clay said softly. "We thought you were trapped inside the case."

"I'm warning you, Luke," I snapped. "Don't jump in any more mummy cases. Don't do anything else crazy. Do you hear me?"

"But I thought we're supposed to try everything," he replied. "Just because you were too big a wimp —"

He didn't finish. We both saw Derek and Margo running across the pavement toward us.

"There you are!" Derek called, grinning. His Marlins cap blew off. He chased it onto the grass.

"Where were you?" I demanded. "Clay and I were so scared. And you — you —"

"We got the whole thing on tape," Margo interrupted. "You were great!"

"Huh? Great?" I sputtered. "But we needed help. We couldn't find you and —"

"You didn't need us. You did a great job," Derek said, pulling the cap carefully over his toupee.

"But Luke could have suffocated!" I screamed.

"No, I couldn't," Luke insisted. "The trapdoor, remember?"

"It's too scary," I cried. "What if the trapdoor didn't open? What if —"

"Let's talk about it later," Margo said, glancing at her watch. "We don't want to waste good taping time."

"Yes. What's next?" Derek asked, eagerly glancing around.

Two little girls walked by with their parents. Both girls were sobbing their heads off. "I don't want to stay here!" one of them wailed, her tearstained face bright red.

"But it's *fun*!" her father argued.

They disappeared around the side of the pyramid.

"Can we do something less scary? Please?" Clay begged.

Luke laughed at Clay. "How about a race?" He grabbed Clay's glasses from his face and took off.

"Hey — give me those!" Clay chased after him.

I hurried after them. Clay caught up with Luke and tackled him around the waist.

"Okay! Okay!" Luke cried. He handed the glasses back. But first he smeared his thumbs over the lenses. "Pretend it's a foggy day!" he told Clay. Then he danced away, laughing like a maniac.

"Where are we?" I asked, glancing around. Across from us, I saw a small store. GRAVEYARD GIFT SHOP, a sign proclaimed. I saw tombstones in the window. And some grinning skulls.

A shiny white building rose up in front of us. A bright red-and-white sign over the door read: HAPPY TOOTH GAME. A giant painting of a grinning molar covered the front wall.

"That looks good," Clay declared. "Come on."

"Sure. Why not? Let's go in," I said, staring at the grinning tooth. "How scary can that be?"

nother smiling tooth was painted on the glass door of the building. I pushed open the door and led the others inside.

We found ourselves in a waiting room. Plastic chairs and couches. A low coffee table piled high with tattered old magazines. A gurgling tropical fish aquarium in one wall.

A female Horror in a white nurse's uniform smiled at us from behind a desk at the front of the room. Above her head, another red-and-white sign: A HAPPY TOOTH IS A HAPPY TOOTH.

"What's *that* supposed to mean?" I whispered to Luke.

He shrugged.

"This looks good," Clay sighed. "Not too scary."

"It looks bor-ring," Luke complained.

"Do you have an appointment?" the nurse asked. She glanced down at a thick appointment book.

"No, we don't," I replied.

"Well, that's no problem." Her smile grew wider. "We have a lot of dentists."

"Huh? Dentists?" I cried. "This is some kind of game — right?"

She stood up. "Follow me."

She pushed open the door behind her and held it for us. We stepped into a bright white room, so bright I shut my eyes.

I heard shrill, whirring sounds all around.

And kids screaming. And crying.

Blinking against the brightness, I stared in shock at an endless row of dental chairs. Gleaming white chairs and spit sinks.

What a horrifying scene!

There had to be at least twenty or thirty chairs, with a screaming patient in almost every one.

White-uniformed dentists hunched over their patients. Drills whistled. The screams and cries couldn't drown out the terrifying drills.

Another nurse strode rapidly toward us. She carried a clipboard in one hand. "The Monster Dentist will see you now," she rasped. "Follow me."

"No. Wait —" I held back.

"Let's g-get out of here," Clay stammered.

Luke stared openmouthed down the endless

row of dentists, whirring drills, and screaming, crying patients.

"Please stop!" a little girl shrieked in the chair closest to us. She struggled to push away her dentist. But he leaned closer, lowering his drill. "It hurts! It hurts!" she wailed. "Stop!"

The boy in the next chair was sobbing at the top of his lungs. "Rinse!" his dentist screamed into his face. "I said *rinse!*"

I raised my eyes from the poor, crying kid to the dentist — and uttered a startled gasp. The dentist really was a monster!

They all were!

They all had hairy, dripping snouts. Yellow fangs curled out from blubbery purple mouths. Pointed ears poked up from the thick black fur that tumbled down over their round, glowing eyes.

They gripped their drills in huge, hairy paws. Lowered their bulky bodies over their screaming, helpless patients.

"You broke my tooth!" a boy wailed halfway down the long row of chairs. "You broke it!"

"Owwwwwww! Help me — somebody!" Another cry, from nearby. "He's drilling my *tongue!*"

I turned my eyes away, swallowing hard. My stomach churned.

"Follow me, please!" the nurse repeated, shouting over the cries and screams and the shrill roar of the drills. "Your Monster Dentist is ready for you now."

"No way!" Clay and I cried in unison.

"We're out of here!" Luke declared.

I spun to the door. Pulled the handle.

The door didn't budge.

Was it just stuck?

I tugged the handle harder.

No. The door was locked.

Clay pounded frantically on the door with his fist. "Let us out! Hey — let us out!"

"No exit," the nurse said sternly.

She motioned with her clipboard — and three big, white-uniformed monsters came lumbering toward us. "These guards will take you to your dentists. Good luck."

"No — please!" I pleaded.

"We changed our minds!" Luke cried.

"Isn't this supposed to be a *game*?" Clay wailed.

The guards grabbed us roughly in their fur-covered paws. We twisted and squirmed. But they were too strong for us. They dragged us down the long row of screaming, crying kids.

"You broke all my teeth!" a boy wailed.

"Help me! Help me!" a girl cried as the Monster Dentist lowered his drill to her face. She clamped her mouth shut and twisted her head away from him.

"Open up — or I'll drill through your *lips*!" the dentist growled.

I turned back, searching for Derek and Margo. Where *were* they? Did they follow us in? Were they hiding somewhere, taping all this?

Weren't they going to help get us out of here?

"No. Please —" I begged as the guard strapped me into a dentist chair near the end of the row. Water gurgled into the white spit sink beside me. I glanced down and saw dark bloodstains on the side of the sink.

"Ohhh — please —" I moaned.

A Monster Dentist popped up beside me. He looked like all the others. He grunted through his dripping snout and snapped his curled fangs together.

"Let me go!" I pleaded. "I don't want to do this!"

"Don't worry," he growled. His booming voice seemed to come from somewhere deep inside him. "I'm a painless dentist."

"Huh? Painless?"

He nodded. "Yes. This won't hurt *me* one bit!"

He reached over my head for the drill.

"A happy tooth is a happy tooth!" he bellowed. "I'll drill some big holes and see how happy your teeth are!"

"No — no! Please!" I begged.

But he pushed a button. The drill roared to life. And with a clumsy, lurching move, he lowered it to my mouth.

bove his snout, the dentist's eyes flashed with excitement. His thick purple lips curled up in an evil grin.

The whirring drill whistled over my face. Closer ... Closer ...

I opened my mouth in a shrill scream.

Then I shot up both fists, frantically trying to push the monster away.

My fists made a *THUNK* sound against his chest.

Gasping for breath, I stared up at him, squirming, twisting, trying to free myself from the heavy leather strap that held me in the chair.

He bent forward again.

I shot my fists up as hard as I could. Another loud *THUNK*.

His chest is solid, I realized. Hard as ... wood!

He uttered a growl from deep inside his chest and slowly lowered the whirring drill again.

I shoved my hands against his face.

"Hey!"

Wood?

Smooth wood. Not skin.

He's made of wood, I realized. He's some kind of robot!

This isn't real! I told myself. The Monster Dentists aren't real.

But what about the screams? The wails and terrified cries of the kids? Are they real?

I didn't have time to find out. Growling angrily, the robot dentist lowered the drill.

I ducked under it, then shoved it away with both hands.

The dentist leaned over me, eyes wide, mouth curled down in an ugly snarl.

With a cry, I grabbed his snout. Grabbed it and twisted it.

His eyes shut. His shoulders slumped.

His hand let go of the drill. His arms lowered themselves stiffly to his sides. His whole body rocked for a moment, then stood still.

Hanging above me, the drill stopped whistling.

I stared up at the dentist, struggling to catch my breath, to slow my pounding heart. He shut down, I realized. The snout must be a turn-off switch.

I shook my head hard, as if trying to force

away the wails and cries of kids and the whistle of drills.

"Robots," I murmured out loud. "Robots."

My hands shook so hard, it took forever to un-hook the strap that held me down. I slid out of the chair and lurched forward on trembling legs.

"Luke? Clay? Where are you?" My voice came out weak and shrill. I knew they couldn't hear me over the noise.

I staggered a few steps down the row of chairs. And saw Luke across from me. He had both hands pressed over his face, but I recognized him from his hair.

A Monster Dentist bent over him, drill in hand, roaring, "I'll drill your lips! I'll drill your lips!"

"No, you won't!" I cried. I dove forward. Grabbed the hairy snout — and twisted. The dentist let out a sound like air escaping a tire, lowered his head and arms, and didn't move.

"Luke — it's okay!" I cried. I had to pry his hands from his face. He stared at me, blinking, swallowing hard.

"The dentists — they're all robots!" I cried.

"I knew that!" he replied.

Typical.

"Of course they're robots," he said. "You didn't think they were real — did you?"

What a liar! If he knew they were robots, why was he covering his face like that?

I wanted to switch the dentist back on and let

him drill on Luke for a while. But instead, I unhooked the strap and tugged Luke out of the chair.

We found Clay a few chairs down. His glasses had fallen into his lap. His eyes were shut tight. His face was drenched in sweat.

I switched off his dentist. Luke shook Clay hard, as if waking him up. "It's okay," he told his friend. "It's not real."

Clay opened his eyes and stared at us as if he didn't recognize us. Luke and I both pulled him from the chair.

I searched frantically for an exit. I couldn't stand listening to the screams and cries for one more second!

Were they real? Were the screaming kids all robots too?

I didn't care.

I spotted a back door across the room, half-hidden by a gray curtain. The three of us raced toward it. We slid past the curtain, pushed the door open, and bolted out.

"Whoa!" I cried out as I nearly ran into Derek and Margo.

"Excellent!" Derek cried, patting his tiny camcorder.

"That was awesome!" Margo declared. "You kids were great. We got the whole thing on tape from that window over there." She pointed.

"But — but —" I sputtered.

"We could have been *wrecked*!" Clay wailed.

"Those dentists . . . all of our teeth . . ." He shuddered.

I shut my eyes, held my breath, and counted to ten. "Calm, Lizzy," I instructed myself. "Be calm . . ."

"It was kind of funny," Luke declared. "I knew those dentists were fake."

"You did not!" I cried angrily. "You were just as scared as Clay and me."

"No way!" Luke insisted.

"I think the kids were all robots too," Derek said, frowning. "So far, everything has been fake. That's not good for the show."

"You're right," Margo agreed. "We want to prove that something terrible is going on here — right? We want to expose how dangerous this park is. So, we need to find some *real* horror."

I swallowed hard. "That was real enough," I murmured, pointing back to the dentist office.

Two Horrors strolled by, carrying brooms, their green tails swinging behind them. Derek and Margo quickly hid their camcorders behind their backs.

"I think we should . . . rest for a while," Clay suggested shakily. He took off his glasses and mopped his sweaty forehead with the sleeve of his T-shirt.

"Real horror," Derek muttered, ignoring him. "Yes. We need to find some real horror. You kids have been resting for too long!" He laughed.

No one else joined in.

"Hey, I'm just trying to cheer you up," Derek grinned. "I want all three of you to survive this place. I really do." He rubbed his chin. "Well . . . maybe *two* out of three!"

Margo shoved him. "You're not funny, Derek. Can't you see? They don't appreciate your sick jokes."

Derek's grin faded. "We do need to find something really dangerous," he murmured. "Or else we don't have a story."

"Hey — how about that place?" Margo cried.

I turned and squinted up at the tall, narrow building across from us, stretching high over the park. Then I read the sign on its gate.

"Oh, no. No way!" I cried.

15

uke went running up to the building entrance. "Stop right there!" I called, chasing after him. "We're not doing this. No way!"

He read the sign out loud: "Elevator Shaft Ride.
World's Fastest Free Fall. It's a Scream. *Drop in
Anytime.*"

I grabbed Luke's shoulders with both hands and
started to march him away. "But it sounds cool!"
he protested.

"Not cool. No way I'm going to go falling down
an elevator shaft," I told him.

"Can't we get something to eat?" Clay whined.

Luke waved a fist in front of Clay's face. "How
about a knuckle sandwich?" he grinned.

"Luke, that's so lame," I said. "Don't you ever
get tired of saying dumb things like that?"

"No," he replied.

"Time is passing," Derek said, checking his watch. "We need to find something really dangerous."

"Hey — there's a food cart," Clay cried.

I turned and saw a short female Horror in a purple apron pushing a small purple cart. The three of us headed over to it. But I stopped when I read the words painted in bright yellow on the side: CARAMEL HEADS.

"What *is* that?" I cried.

The Horror motioned to the cart. "Shrunken heads on a stick," she replied, "covered in caramel."

"Yuck." I felt my stomach churn.

"The outside is very sweet," the Horror told us. "The head inside is kind of sour. Except for the eyeballs."

She held one out to us. It looked like a caramel apple. Except beneath the thick, gooey layer of brown caramel, I could see two closed eyes and the bump of a nose.

Clay groaned. I covered my mouth.

"That head — it isn't real, right?" Luke asked.

"Right," the Horror answered. And then she burst out laughing. "We would never use real heads here in HorrorLand — would we?" she asked sarcastically.

She raised the stick toward us. "How many do you want? One for each of you? Or more? You know, two heads are better than one." She laughed again.

We didn't laugh. I squinted at the caramel-covered head. At the closed eyes, the ears poking through the brown goo ... the lips ...

And then I let out a gasp as the lips parted. Through the layer of caramel, I saw the mouth open. Saw it move. Saw the tiny lips silently form the words: "Help ... me ..."

"We don't want any!" The scream burst from my mouth.

I spun around searching for the Stranges. Were they taping this? Did they see the lips move on the shrunken head?

No. They were gone. They had vanished again.

The Horror pushed her cart away, chuckling to herself, her tail wagging behind her.

Clay grabbed my arm, his face pale, his chin quivering. "Lizzy, did you see that? Was that real?" he whispered.

I shrugged. "I don't know. We've got to find Derek and Margo. They disappeared again, and we don't know what they want us to do next."

"Maybe they went up ahead," Luke suggested. He began half skipping, half dancing down the path.

"Luke — wait up!" I called after him. "We're supposed to stick together."

We made our way past the dark towers of Dracula's Castle and then something called the Insect Garden. I could hear loud buzzing and snapping sounds on the other side of the tall hedge. I shivered. I really didn't want to see what was over there.

The path curved around to a narrow, slow moving river. "Check it out!" Luke cried, pointing to a bunch of small wooden crafts bobbing in the water. "The coffin ride is still here. Remember that?"

I read the sign: COFFIN CRUISE. A RELAXING FLOAT TO THE GRAVE.

"Of course I remember that horrible ride!" I exclaimed. Last summer, our whole family had floated down the river in coffins. A slow, relaxing ride — until the lids slammed shut on us, and we discovered the coffins were filled with spiders.

"I'm never going back on that," Clay declared. "Never!"

"Where are the Stranges?" I asked impatiently. "Why do they keep disappearing all the time? It really isn't fair."

"Yeah. They promised they'd watch us," Clay agreed.

We followed the path up from the river. Now we were walking in the shadow of an endless brick wall. Tall trees rose up behind the wall, blocking the sunlight.

The air grew colder. I didn't see anyone else around here.

"I-I don't think Derek and Margo came this

way," I stammered. "I think we've walked too far. We should turn back."

"Let's just see what's up ahead," Luke insisted. He was walking backwards, doing a hopping dance step.

And he backed right into a huge, hulking Horror, who appeared out of nowhere.

"Hey!" Luke cried out in surprise. He stumbled away from the Horror.

The Horror glared at us sternly. He was a *mountain* — at least eight feet tall! His green arms were bare under his purple uniform, showing off biceps as big as volleyballs!

"I — I think we're lost," I told him.

He nodded. "Yes, you *are* lost!" he boomed.

Before we could move, three more hulking, muscle-bound Horrors moved out from an opening in the wall. They circled us. Spread out. And raised a black mesh net high over our heads.

"Hey — what's the big idea?" Luke demanded.

"We're fishing," the giant Horror murmured.

I let out a cry as they pulled the net down, trapping all three of us inside.

"What are you *doing*?" I shrieked. "Let us out!"

The Horrors didn't say a word. They tightened the net around us.

We struggled. Thrashed our arms. Tried to pull back.

But they dragged us up the path. Pushed us and pulled us along the curving wall.

"Where are you taking us?" Clay shrieked. "Why won't you answer?"

I peered back through the net, struggling to see if the Stranges were behind us.

No sign of them.

"Let us go!"

"You can't do this!"

They ignored our shouts. One of them shoved me hard from behind. I stumbled through a narrow opening in the wall.

"Stop it! Let us out!" I screamed.

"Keep moving," the huge Horror growled.

They dragged us into darkness along a narrow brick walkway between two walls. Through a low door. And then down steep stone steps, wet and slippery, slick with a coating of green.

"Where are you taking us?" I demanded angrily.

"Our parents will be looking for us," Luke declared. "They were right behind us. We're going to tell them —"

"You won't be telling them anything," a Horror muttered, giving me another push.

"Heyyyyy —" I cried out as we toppled down the rest of the stairs. The stones were hard and damp. The three of us landed in a heap at the bottom, tangled in the net.

As we scrambled to our feet, the Horrors pulled the net away.

"Please . . . ," Clay begged them. "Please . . ." I

saw his chin quivering. His eyes were wide with fear.

My legs were trembling as I stood up. I bent and pulled Luke to his feet. Then I gazed around.

We were in a low stone room, completely bare. A torch on the wall sent flickering shadows over the stone floor. A narrow doorway on the back wall revealed only darkness. I could hear the steady *DRIP DRIP DRIP* of water from somewhere nearby.

The Horrors turned and stepped back as another Horror swept into the room. His purple cape swirled behind him. His head was covered by a long black mask. Two bright yellow eyes peered out at us through narrow eye slits in the mask.

"Here are your volunteers, sir," the huge Horror boomed.

The masked Horror stared at us, tugging at the neck of his cape with one hand. "Three of them," he muttered to himself.

"Wh-who are you?" I managed to choke out.

"I'm the Dungeon Master, of course," he replied in a hoarse, breathy voice.

"Why did you bring us here?" I demanded.

"You have to let us go!" Luke cried. "We don't want to visit the dungeon. You can't make us!"

"Let us go!" Clay echoed.

The Dungeon Master ignored us. He turned to the powerful Horror. "Was anyone with them?"

"No," the Horror replied.

"Did anyone see you bring them here?" the Dungeon Master asked.

The big Horror shook his head. "No. No one around. No one saw us."

"Good," the Dungeon Master rasped from under his black mask. He clasped his hands together and cracked his knuckles loudly, all of them at once.

I shuddered. It sounded like bones breaking.

"Good," he repeated, turning to us. "I'm so glad to have company. I was getting bored."

16

"**Y**ou can't do this!" I cried in a trembling voice. "What do you plan to do?"

The Dungeon Master snickered. "Well . . . this place is called the Dungeon of No Return," he said. "Does that give you a clue?"

All three of us stared at him. "This . . . this is a joke — right?" Luke finally said.

Behind the black mask, the Dungeon Master's yellow eyes flashed. "Yes," he rasped. "But the joke is on you." He turned to the other Horrors. "Let's get them down the stairs," he ordered.

The grim-faced Horrors moved quickly. They forced us down another curving stone stairway.

We had no choice. Holding onto the damp wall with one hand, we made our way down. The air grew colder. A stale, sour odor rose up to greet us.

I shivered. In the dim yellow light, I could see my breath steam in front of me. Down below, I heard the steady drip of water, echoing dully against the stone walls. And from somewhere in the distance, a long, sad moan. A human moan.

"Our parents will be looking for us," I called to the Horrors behind us. "You won't be able to keep us here."

"Be quiet and keep moving. You're almost there," one of them replied gruffly.

Where *are* Derek and Margo? I wondered. Did they lose us? Or do they know we are down here? Are they hiding somewhere, taping this whole thing?

If the Stranges are here, they should help us, I told myself. The other frightening activities might have been jokes. But this seemed so real. Too real . . .

"Ohhh!" I slipped on a wet step. I grabbed the cold, rough wall to keep from falling. Green mossy goo clung to my hands.

"Let us out of here!" I pleaded weakly. "You can't keep us in your stupid dungeon!"

The Horrors didn't reply.

We stepped into a large, high-ceilinged chamber filled with equipment. Torture equipment. Nooses hung from the ceiling. Chains with handcuffs were attached to the wall in pairs.

I stumbled up against a high wooden wheel covered with metal spikes. Across from me, I saw a small cage, also filled with spikes.

A loud scream made me jump and cry out. A scream of pain, of terror. It was followed by another shrill scream, weaker this time.

The Dungeon Master swept into the room. "Pay no attention to those pitiful bleats," he said. He motioned to the far wall. "It is another volunteer enjoying our hospitality. I'm afraid he is a very bad sport."

He pushed his cape behind him. "You are admiring my torture chamber," he said. "Let me demonstrate my collection of thumbscrews."

He held up a small metal device. "This fits over your thumb," he said. "Then I tighten this screw. Tighten it . . . tighten it . . ."

I choked.

He laughed. "Yes. It hurts a little. But after a while in my dungeon, you get used to pain."

Luke stared down at his thumb, then raised his eyes to the thumbscrew. "Are you . . . going to put that on us?" he asked in a tiny voice.

The Dungeon Master shook his head. "I have other plans for you. Something more exciting."

The three Horrors pushed us forward. "Step onto that platform," the big one ordered.

He gave me a hard shove. We stepped onto a small square platform cut into the floor. As soon as we stood on it, it started to lower.

A trapdoor, I realized.

Stone scraped against stone. The platform bumped as it moved down, a few inches at a time. I struggled to keep my balance.

Where was it taking us?

"Have you ever seen a ferret?" the Dungeon Master called.

Huh? A ferret? The little rodenty animal?

"My friend has a ferret," Luke replied.

"What does it look like?" Clay asked.

"It has light tan fur and a really skinny body and short legs," Luke told him.

"But around its eyes it has dark black fur," I added. "Like a mask."

"Is it big?" Clay asked.

"It's about this big." Luke spread his hands two feet apart.

"Furry, skinny, short, a mask, medium-sized," Clay recited a list. "That doesn't sound so bad," he said nervously.

"Right?"

"Not so bad?" the Dungeon Master snickered. "Have you ever seen a *hungry* ferret?"

We didn't have time to reply. The platform bounced as it hit the floor.

Clay toppled off. He fell hard, landing on his side on the damp stones. Luke and I jumped off. Luke helped Clay up.

I gazed around quickly. My eyes stopped at a sign on the wall in front of us: FEED THE FERRETS.

"Oh, no! Look!" Luke grabbed my arm.

I turned in the direction he was gazing.

And saw tiny black eyes — *hundreds* of glowing eyes — staring back at us.

A chittering sound rose up. The click of rodent feet on stone as the ferrets shifted and started to move.

Hungry ferrets, I thought. *Hungry ferrets . . . feed the ferrets . . . feed the hungry ferrets . . .* The terrifying words repeated in my mind like an ugly chant.

"Quick — run!" I gasped.

But we were backed against the wall.

Nowhere to run. Nowhere to move.

Flashes of gray. Sleek, furry heads. Clicking teeth. And those cold, darkly glowing eyes . . .

Chittering, clicking, snapping their teeth, the ferrets stampeded.

We all screamed and backed up against the wall.

Pressed helplessly against the cold stone wall, we watched them attack.

"Nooooooo!" A terrified scream escaped my throat.

Those round black eyes! Those glowing marble eyes! Those *hungry* eyes!

Shrill shrieks rose up from the ferrets as they leaped at us.

"Ohhhh!" I covered my eyes.

I could feel the warm, furry bodies swarm around my legs.

"Get away!" I yelled, thrashing my feet, kicking at the hungry creatures.

Hundreds of sharp teeth gnawed on my jeans. "Stop!" I hollered. "Leave us alone!"

The ferrets pressed in tighter. They crawled over each other, in a mad frenzy to attack us.

Their shrieks grew shriller.

"They're going to eat us alive!" Clay wailed.

"Oooo," I let out a moan as a ferret leaped up from the hungry throng. With a gaping mouth and teeth bared, it flung itself at me.

I jerked to the side to dodge it — and my elbow bumped something. A tiny button on the stone.

I heard a whirring hum as the wall began to move.

"Huh?" I opened my eyes in time to see the stone wall spin.

It spun completely around, pushing the three of us out of the dungeon. Pushing us outside.

Stunned, I heard a dull *THUD*. Another. Another. Dozens of loud *BUMPS* on the other side of the wall.

The hungry ferrets were attacking, leaping at the wall, throwing themselves, desperate to get to us.

"Whoa." I squinted into the sunlight. Luke and Clay appeared dazed but okay.

"A . . . close . . . one . . .," Clay murmured.

"Helll-llo. Those ferrets were real!" Luke declared, shaking his head. "And they were really hungry."

I blinked, still waiting for my heart to stop pounding. "What if I hadn't bumped that button?" I gasped. "What if . . ." My voice trailed off.

I spun away from the wall. I knew I'd never forget the sight of those glowing black ferret eyes. I'd never be able to erase the sound of their ratlike bodies thudding against the stone from my memory.

Talk about close calls!

I shielded my eyes with one hand and searched for the Stranges. No sign of them.

"Where are they?" I wailed. "I've had enough of HorrorLand. I don't care about their stupid TV show. I want to get out of here!"

"Me too," Clay agreed.

"Maybe they're hiding," Luke suggested. "Getting it all on tape."

"I don't care," I snapped. "This place is too dangerous."

Clay had his frightened owl expression on his round, pale face. "Maybe Derek and Margo are in trouble," he whispered. "Maybe they got dragged into a dungeon or something, the way we did."

"I don't care," I moaned. "I want *out* of here. I think we should —"

"Check that out!" Luke interrupted, pointing across a grassy circle.

I squinted into the sunlight at a small, black-curtained stage with rows of benches in front of it. Huge paintings of white rabbits being pulled from top hats rose up on both sides of the little stage.

Luke pulled me toward the sign at the side of the dark-curtained theater. AMAZ-O THE MAGICIAN. APPEARING — AND DISAPPEARING! — DAILY.

"Huh? What's *he* doing here?" I cried. "He's a very famous magician." I gazed at Amaz-O's photo on the sign. He wore a cape and a glittery bow tie. He had black hair tumbling down from a shiny top hat, flashing dark eyes, and a broad, mischievous smile.

I watched two families take seats on the benches. Several other kids were already sitting there, waiting for Amaz-O's show.

"Maybe we should wait for the Stranges at the magic show," I suggested. "We'll be safe there. Lots of people around."

"And we can watch the show!" Luke gushed. "He's a great magician. I've seen him on TV."

"It's not too scary, is it?" Clay asked. He was still pale and shaky from our trip to the dungeon.

"It's just magic tricks," Luke told him, trotting toward the stage. "Come on."

Clay and I followed Luke. The three of us took seats in the third row.

It felt good to sit down. I took a deep breath and let it out slowly. The little theater was quickly filling up with kids and their parents.

I felt a lot safer surrounded by people. But I kept turning back, searching the area for the Stranges.

What was keeping them?

The afternoon sun floated high in the sky. The air felt wet and sticky. No breeze at all.

I mopped my forehead with the back of my hand. I could go for a cold drink, I thought. But all the food carts we'd seen had been so totally gross and disgusting.

A loud musical fanfare interrupted my thoughts.

A loudspeaker boomed to life, and a deep voice announced: "Ladies and gentlemen, boys and girls, HorrorLand is proud to present the Master of Magic — Amaz-O the Magician!"

Amaz-O strutted onstage to another fanfare. As the audience clapped and cheered, he swept his sparkly cape around and took several deep bows.

Another fanfare. Smiling at the audience, the magician removed his top hat and began pulling things from it. His smile never faded as he pulled out an endless chain of colorful handkerchiefs.

Then he reached in deeper and began to pull out red rubber balls. Dozens of them. Then he twirled the hat, tapped it twice with a short black wand — and began pulling out bunny rabbits. Rabbit after rabbit came up from the hat as the audience cheered.

The little stage filled with bunnies, hopping uncertainly in circles, bumping into each other.

"All empty!" Amaz-O declared finally. He raised the top hat high in the air and smashed it flat with his other hand. "Oh, wait!" He squinted at the flattened hat. "I forgot something in there!"

He punched the hat back to its shape. Then he began pulling pigeons from it.

The audience cheered. They really went wild as pigeon after pigeon came out of the hat.

"How does he do that?" Clay asked my brother.

Luke shrugged. "I think he's got them up his sleeve or something."

Amaz-O performed trick after trick. He was really good. Even sitting so close, in the third row, it was impossible to see how he did his tricks.

But I wasn't really in the mood for magic tricks. The day had been too upsetting, too frightening. And I was beginning to worry about Derek and Margo.

I didn't pay much attention to Amaz-O's show. I kept turning back, hoping to find the Stranges coming for us.

I was only half listening when Amaz-O pointed to me. "Yes. You," he was saying.

"Huh?" My mouth dropped open.

He motioned me forward. "Hurry up. You're my volunteer."

"But —" I started to protest.

Beside me, Luke and Clay were laughing. "Go, girl!" Luke cried. "Hurry, Lizzy — get up there!"

I was *not* in the mood for this. But before I realized it, I was standing onstage beside Amaz-O, my knees shaking, wondering what kind of trick I was in.

I didn't have to wait long. I heard a loud, unfriendly growl. The black curtain behind us lifted. I turned to see two enormous tigers pacing in a tall metal cage.

"It's my famous tiger cage trick!" Amaz-O declared. He grinned at me, eyes twinkling. "One of us is going into that tiger cage. Can you guess which one?"

My heart skipped a beat. One of the tigers angrily slashed a claw against the cage bars. The other one pulled back its lips and bared its teeth.

"Don't worry about them," Amaz-O cried, still grinning. "They're just angry because I ate their breakfast this morning!" He patted my back. "Maybe you can be *lunch*!"

I heard Luke and Clay laughing loudly in the audience. I tried to hold back. But Amaz-O guided me firmly up to the cage door.

Both tigers roared and bared their teeth. They watched eagerly as Amaz-O unbolted the door and started to pull it open.

"Our brave volunteer will enter the tiger cage — and the tigers will disappear into thin air!" Amaz-O proclaimed to the audience.

"Uh . . . this is safe — right?" I whispered.

He nodded. "Just keep in mind one important thing," he whispered back. "When you're in there, don't let them see that you're afraid. They can smell fear a mile away. Whatever you do, be brave."

He pulled open the cage door with one hand — and shoved me inside with the other.

"No, wait — please!" I cried.

I heard the door clang shut behind me.

Eyeing me coldly, the tigers lowered their heads as if getting ready to attack. They growled softly. One of them pawed the cage floor.

"Wait!" I cried out as darkness fell over me.

The curtain! Amaz-O had lowered the curtain.

Total blackness now. I could hear the tigers' low growls, their heavy breathing. But I couldn't see them.

And then . . . I staggered back as I heard an angry roar.

The thud of heavy paws.

Now I could feel the tigers' hot breath on my face.

I backed away. Pressed myself against the cold bars of the tiny cage.

The tigers let out another roar. Deafening this time.

"Let me out of here!" I screamed.

"Pull up the curtain!" Amaz-O's frightened cry from the front of the stage made me gasp. "Pull it up! Something is wrong!" Amaz-O screeched. "Hurry! Something is horribly wrong!"

I shut my eyes.

And dropped to my knees on the cage floor.

And waited for the attack. For the pain.

Another angry roar made me cry out.

I heard gasps from the audience. And then applause.

I opened my eyes. And blinked, startled by the brightness.

The curtain had been lifted.

The tigers were gone. Vanished into thin air — just as Amaz-O had promised.

My whole body trembled.

Why didn't Amaz-O tell me what was going to happen? Why didn't he warn me?

The tiger trick was like everything else at HorrorLand — too frightening to be fun. Too dangerous. Too real . . .

I grabbed the cage bars and pulled myself to my feet. Amaz-O had left the stage. The show was over. People were walking out of the little theater.

I swallowed hard and gazed around the cage. I couldn't see a trapdoor in the floor. How had the tigers disappeared?

"Hey!" I tried to call out. But my throat was still tight with fear.

"Hey — is anyone going to let me out of here?" I managed to shout. "Hey — anyone?"

I held on to the bars and peered out. "Hey — I'm still locked in here!"

I couldn't see anyone backstage. In front of me, the rows of benches stood empty.

"Hey — Luke? Clay? Where are you?" I called. "Somebody — get me out of here!"

19

A powerful-looking Horror in a guard's uniform squinted up at me from the theater floor. "Hey — show's over!" he barked. "You've got to leave!"

"They forgot about me!" I cried.

"Get moving," he ordered. "Show's over. Everybody out."

"But I'm locked in here!" I protested.

"No, you're not." He scowled at me.

"Excuse me?" I moved to the cage door. And pushed the bars. The door slid open.

Not locked.

"Uh . . . thanks," I uttered. But the Horror had already left.

Taking a deep breath, I stepped out of the cage. Jumped down from the stage. Called out to Luke and Clay.

No sign of them.

I stopped in front of the big bunny posters out-side the theater. "Luke? Clay? Hey!"

Two boys walked along the hedge, carrying cara-mel heads on sticks, licking at them as they walked. I blinked, thinking it was Luke and Clay. But no.

I shouted their names again.

I ran along the walkway past the theater, searching in every direction. Then I ran back. No sign of them.

Something is wrong, I muttered to myself. They should be here. They wouldn't wander off without me.

Where should I look for them? I wondered. Is there a lost-and-found? Maybe they found the Stranges. Maybe they're all waiting for me at the front gate.

I spotted a map of the park tacked to a wall. I hurried up to it. My eyes swept over the map. Words beside a red arrow read: YOU ARE HERE. YOU ARE NOT GOING ANYWHERE.

"Not funny," I murmured. I desperately tried to figure out which path would lead me to the en-trance of the park. I traced my finger along the map. Then I took off.

I passed the Coffin Cruise on the river. Then a ride called SWIM THE RAPIDS: LEAKY RAFT RIDE. I trotted past a sign that read: SCREAM CLUB. I could hear kids screaming their heads off inside the clubhouse building.

The afternoon sun was beginning to lower itself behind the trees. Long shadows stretched along the path. A few kids walked by, looking tired and upset. But the park was nearly deserted.

My side started to ache, and I had to slow down. I heard the clatter of bowling pins. A sign in front of a long, low building read: HEADLESS BOWLING. I didn't stop to see what *that* was about.

Where are they? I asked myself for the hundredth time. Where did Luke and Clay disappear to?

It seemed to take forever, but I finally jogged out onto the wide, concrete plaza in the front of the park. I could see the small office building to my right. The entrance gates stood up ahead.

"Hey!" I stopped short when I saw the Stranges near the gate. "Hey!" I tried to call out to them. But I'd been running so long, I couldn't catch my breath.

I stopped short, holding my side. And gaped in shock. What was happening?

Four Horrors had Derek and Margo surrounded. They were pushing them roughly toward the exit.

The Stranges were screaming angrily and gesturing wildly. They were trying to break away from the Horrors.

"Wait!" I cried.

I watched two Horrors grab the Stranges' camcorders from their hands. The Horrors angrily tossed the video cameras to the concrete and stomped on them.

Then they shoved Derek and Margo out of the park and slammed the gate shut.

"No — wait!" I cried frantically. "Stop! Come back!"

Shouting, waving my arms, I ran to the gate.

The four Horrors moved to block my way.

"I need them!" I cried breathlessly. "Derek! Margo! Wait! Please!"

I tried to run past the Horrors and get to the gate. But they moved quickly. They surrounded me.

"They're out of here. They won't be coming back," one of the Horrors growled.

Another Horror brought his green face close to mine and sneered, "You got a problem with that?"

20

"They broke the rules," a Horror growled. "They had to leave."

The other Horror still had his face inches from mine. "Maybe you have to leave too," he whispered. He grabbed my wrist.

"No!" I cried. I jerked my hand free. "I have to find my brother and his friend! I can't leave!"

"Time to go," the Horror insisted.

"No! Not without the boys!" I screamed. "They're lost!"

All four Horrors burst out laughing. "Don't make us laugh. We have chapped lips!" one of them sneered.

He pulled open the gate and motioned for me to leave. "Out."

"No!" I insisted. "No way!"

He grabbed for me again.

I spun away and started to run. Gasping, my chest heaving, I tore through the plaza and back onto a narrow trail.

Were they chasing after me?

Yes!

"Red alert!" one of them yelled to another group of Horrors. "Red alert! I want her brought in!"

Oh, no! I thought. Soon, every Horror in the park will be out to catch me.

Beads of sweat ran down my face. But I felt cold, so cold. Chills ran down my back. My legs felt rubbery and weak.

"Luke! Clay!" I shouted their names.

Where were they? I had to find them — before the Horrors caught up to me.

I was all alone now, all alone in this terrifying park. The Stranges were gone. It was up to me now. Up to me to find the boys and get us safely away from this nightmare place.

"Luke! Clay!"

I ran full speed through Zombie Town, dark even though the sun was still shining. Past the Bat Barn and the Doom Slides.

My heart pounding, I ran past a small gift shop. Dozens of green Horror costumes hung on display.

Why would anyone buy a Horror costume? I wondered.

I kept running, calling for Luke and Clay. I felt more frightened with each step. I kept telling myself not to panic — but it was too late for that.

Too late . . . too late . . .

When I do find them, how will we get out of here? I asked myself. And how will we get home?

One thing at a time, Lizzy, I scolded myself.

I turned a corner — and saw two Horrors heading toward me. "There she is!" one of them cried. They lowered their horns and started to run.

With a frightened gasp, I pulled back around the corner and took off in another direction. My shoes pounded the brick street.

I turned and headed behind a building called Howl House. Then I turned again, into a narrow alley. I came out of the alley and headed toward the river.

My chest felt about ready to explode. My head throbbed.

I glanced back and saw that I had lost them.

But I knew that more Horrors would be after me.

Running hard, I followed the path that curved along the water. I stopped short — nearly toppled over — when I heard screams.

Frightened screams.

I recognized the voices. Luke and Clay!

My eyes swept over a sign: VULTURE BEACH. PLEASE FEED THE VULTURES.

Another frightened shriek.

"I'm coming, Luke!" I screamed breathlessly.

I ducked under the sign. Onto a small, sandy beach.

And saw the two boys — chained down. On their backs. Handcuffed. Chained to wooden stakes that poked up from the sand.

Blue-black shadows swooped over them.

"Lizzy — help! Help us!" Luke wailed, struggling against the chains.

"Hurry —" Clay pleaded. "The Horrors — they chained us here!"

The shadows rolled over the sand, over the struggling boys.

I raised my eyes — and saw what was casting them.

Vultures.

Enormous, black vultures . . . swooping . . . lower and lower.

Their black wings stretched wide. Their bald white heads craned. Cawing and croaking hungrily.

Swooping lower . . .

Circling Luke and Clay. Preparing to feed.

21

"Lizzy — help! Hurry!"

I was frozen, staring up in horror at the ugly, swooping vultures.

But Luke's desperate cry stirred me to action.

I plunged across the sand to the boys. Dropping to my knees, I tugged frantically at the chains.

"Get us out! Get us out!" Luke repeated, his eyes on the huge, circling birds.

I heard a hard *BUMP* on the sand, close behind me. A loud, ugly squawk.

I glanced back and saw that a vulture had landed. It flapped its dark wings and tilted its head. And came darting across the sand toward us.

BUMP.

Another big bird landed heavily.

"Hurry!" Luke begged.

The two vultures opened their curved beaks and uttered hungry cries.

I tugged at the handcuff around Luke's wrist. "Don't make a fist!" I instructed him. "Keep your hand loose. I think you can slide it out."

"They're going to *eat* us!" Clay wailed. "That's what vultures do — right? They're going to eat us alive!"

I didn't have time to answer. I heard the heavy beating of wings.

"Hey!" I cried out as a vulture dove at me from behind.

I fell over and it shot its beak at Luke. Snapped at his neck. I heard a harsh shriek and it snapped again.

"Nooo!" I wailed.

I thrust out both hands and shoved the squawking bird's side. The feathers felt hot and dry.

The bird flapped its wings frantically. Flapped until it regained its balance. Then dove at us again.

It batted its heavy wings against my face. Snapped its beak at my hair.

"Get away!" I cried, shielding my head with my hands.

Its wings thrashed against the back of my neck. Again, its powerful beak snapped just above me.

"No!" I screamed again waving my arms madly at the diving bird.

THUMP.

Another vulture landed on the beach. Another one swooped low, preparing to attack.

"What am I going to do?" I screamed. "I can't fight them all!"

The first vulture let out an ugly shriek and swooped onto me again.

Its wings beat against my face. I couldn't see . . . couldn't breathe.

Squawking and crying, all the vicious birds attacked.

Beating us with their wings. Snapping their powerful beaks.

Batting them away with both hands, I lost my balance and fell to the sand.

Two vultures swooped over me and dove at Luke and Clay.

"Help me, Lizzy!" Luke screamed. "They're trying to poke my eyes out!"

"No! Noooo!" Clay shrieked. He thrashed his head wildly from side to side, trying to dodge the attacking birds.

I grabbed two handfuls of sand. And with a furious cry, heaved them at the diving vultures.

The big birds stopped. They drew back. Sand clung to the top of their bony heads and the feathers on their backs.

I tossed another handful of sand.

The birds backed up. I could see that they didn't like the sand attacks.

Two vultures stood at the shoreline, still as statues. They hunched tensely with their wings slightly raised, watching the battle. A silent audience.

I heaved more sand. Then I turned back to Luke. I held the handcuff. "Slide your hand out!" I shrieked, my eye on the angry vultures. "You can do it! There's enough room!"

"Yes!" he cried happily as his hand slid free. He turned and worked his other hand free.

I hopped over him and set to work on Clay's handcuffs.

Behind me, vultures squawked loudly. I turned to see them raise their wings . . . lower their heads . . .

"Noooo!" I let out a wild cry as the ugly birds attacked. Swooping furiously at us. Swiping their beaks. Snapping. Flapping wildly. Sending up a dark cloud of sand and pebbles and feathers.

"Clay — hurry!" I moaned.

I shoved a squawking vulture off my head. Its talons pulled at my hair. Nearly pulled me over. It dropped to the sand. Spun around. And dove at Luke.

"Okay!" Clay cried. He slid his hands free. I helped him to his feet.

"Let's get out of here!" I cried, pulling him by the hand.

The vultures snapped. Dove at us. A shrieking

bird flew into Luke, sending him sprawling to the sand.

Luke staggered to his feet.

And we ran.

Ran as fast and hard as we could.

Ran till we left the squawking birds behind us.

"Those birds must be *starving!*" I cried. "Vultures usually don't attack living creatures!"

"Which way?" Luke gasped. "How do we get out of here?"

"Oh, no!" I turned and cried out. I saw a group of eight or ten Horrors running down the beach toward us.

I spun in the other direction. "This way!" I told the boys.

But another group of Horrors ran along the shoreline in *that* direction.

Trapped, I thought.

Now we'll *all* be vulture food.

"No!" I wasn't going to give up. "Let's go this way!"

I took off, back toward the path that had brought me to the beach. The boys followed close behind.

"Where are we going? Why are they chasing us?" Luke demanded.

"Later," I gasped. I led them into the narrow alley behind Howl House. We could hear screams and cries from inside the building.

"Stop!" an angry voice called.

I turned to see four Horrors advancing on us from the end of the alley.

I took off, around to the front of Howl House and then down a wide path that appeared to be empty.

But it quickly filled with Horrors. When they spotted us, they started waving furiously, shouting for us to freeze.

"I think every Horror in HorrorLand is after us!" I gasped. "We've got to get away."

"But how?" Luke cried.

I grabbed both boys and shoved them around the side of a tall hedge. "This way," I told them.

"But — why?" Luke demanded. "How are we going to escape?"

Suddenly, I had an idea.

22

led them to the gift shop where I had seen the Horror costumes. There were no Horrors behind the counter. They were probably out with all the others, trying to capture us.

We grabbed costumes off the rack and scrambled into them.

"This mask doesn't fit!" Clay complained. I adjusted my mask and turned to him. His mask was too big. The horns fell over his face.

I tossed him another mask.

"They'll know we're not real Horrors," Luke muttered. "This isn't going to work."

"Well, if you have any better ideas, tell us!" I snapped.

He shook his head.

"Try to walk like a Horror," I told them. "Swing your tail. Like this." I demonstrated. "And mainly, act calm. Don't act suspicious. Walk slowly and calmly."

"Okay, okay," Luke replied impatiently. He glanced out to the road. "Where are we going?"

"To the front gate," I told him. "We won't be safe until we're out of the park."

"And where are the Stranges?" Clay asked.

"They were caught with their camcorders. The Horrors threw them out," I said. "Come on. Follow me."

We didn't get far.

We stepped out onto the path and four big, powerful-looking Horrors surrounded us.

"Where do you think *you're* going?" their leader snarled.

23

I stared at them through the mask. My heart nearly stopped beating. My legs suddenly felt too weak to hold me up.

"Uh . . . well . . ." I hesitated.

"We're looking for those three kids," Luke chimed in.

Yessss! Thank you, Luke, I thought.

"Yeah. We thought we saw them go this way," he continued.

Luke, stop right there, I thought, holding my breath. Don't go too far.

The leader of the four Horrors frowned at us. "No way," he growled.

Oh, no. We're caught, I realized. He isn't buying Luke's story.

"No way," the Horror repeated sharply. "You're not supposed to be searching this section. This is *our* section." He motioned to his three partners. "Our section."

"Sorry," I burst in quickly. "We didn't mean to. We were following the path and —"

"Check out the beach," the Horror ordered. "Stay out of our section, hear? We've got it covered."

"Okay," I said, sighing happily. The boys and I hurried away. I could feel the Horrors' eyes on us as we moved. I didn't look back.

We passed two other groups of Horrors as we made our way to the front. They nodded to us, but didn't speak.

When the front gate came into view, we ducked into the shadow of a building. "How are we going to get past the Horror at the gate?" Luke asked. "We can't just walk out."

"Why not?" Clay demanded. "We're so close. Let's just say we're going for a walk or something."

I peered out at the Horror. He stood stiffly in his little booth, his eyes sweeping back and forth over the front of the park.

"Luke is right," I told Clay. "Maybe the Horrors never leave HorrorLand. We don't know for sure if they do or not. If we try to walk out, we'll be caught for sure."

All three of us watched the gate guard.

"So close . . .," Luke murmured. "We're so close to escaping." He raised his eyes. "Can we climb the fence?"

"Too tall," Clay replied. "And maybe it's electrified."

"I have an idea," I told them. I took a deep breath. "Wait here."

I took another deep breath and walked up to the ticket booth. The Horror turned slowly to me. He appeared old, his green face drawn and wrinkled. One of the horns on top of his head was cracked. His tail dragged on the ground.

"How is it going?" he rasped. "Did they catch those three kids?"

I nodded. "Yes. I heard they caught them," I told him. "They sent me over so you could take a break."

He squinted at me. "So early?"

I shrugged. "I don't mind. Go take your rest. It's quiet out here today."

He stared at me some more through his watery eyes.

Did he believe me? Would he leave the gate?

Yes! He shoved a ticket puncher and a few other items into a leather bag. Then he gave me a little wave and shuffled off in the direction of the office.

I waited, holding my breath, until he disappeared into the building. Then I waved frantically for the boys to join me.

I didn't need to wave. They were already running full speed across the front plaza.

Seconds later, we burst through the gate — and kept running. Across the gravel parking lot, nearly empty now. Then under the big billboard at the front of the park and onto the road.

"We're out!" Luke cried gleefully, pumping his fists in the air. "We're safe!" He pulled off his mask and did a little dance.

Clay and I didn't celebrate with him. "How will we get home?" Clay asked me in a tiny voice. He tugged off his mask. Sweat poured down his forehead, onto his glasses.

"Uh . . . we'll find a phone," I told him. "And we'll call my mom and dad. There's got to be a house or a store or something on this road."

We trotted along the side of the road. The sun had started to lower itself behind the trees. Long blue shadows stretched over us. The air grew cooler.

I didn't hear the van until it pulled up beside us.

I cried out, startled, as the driver's door swung open.

We're caught! I thought.

Derek Strange climbed out from behind the wheel. I was never so glad to see anyone in my life!

"You're okay!" he cried happily. He grabbed both of my hands and squeezed them.

Luke and Clay cheered and jumped up and down happily.

Margo came running around the side of the van. "We were so worried!" she cried. "How did you escape?"

107

"It wasn't easy!" I exclaimed.

"Every Horror in the park came after us," Luke told them.

"Thank goodness you're okay!" Derek sighed. "They spotted our cameras and threw us out of the park. We searched for another way to get back in. But we couldn't find one."

"We were so worried," Margo repeated, shaking her head. "Quick — get in the van. Let's get away from this horrible place. As far away as we can."

That sounded good to me. We all piled back into the van.

"You kids are amazing!" Derek declared. "How did you ever get away? I want to hear the whole story."

He put the van in gear, and we took off.

I settled back in the seat, still feeling shaky, my heart still racing. I took a deep breath and watched the trees pass by outside the van window.

Whoa . . . wait . . .

Something wrong here . . .

Derek turned the van around and lowered his foot on the gas pedal. The van shot forward. The trees blurred past.

The HorrorLand sign came into view.

"Stop!" I shrieked. "What are you *doing*? Why are you driving us back to HorrorLand?"

We drove under the sign, into the parking lot.

"Let us out!" I screamed. "Let us out — now!"

I grabbed the door handle and tugged it hard. But Derek had locked the doors.

He screeched to a stop at the front gate. Out the window, I saw dozens of Horrors running eagerly toward us. They surrounded the van. Through the closed window, I could hear their excited, happy chattering.

Derek unlocked the doors. He and Margo climbed out.

"What are we going to do?" Luke wailed.

I didn't have time to answer.

Horrors slid open the door. Green hands grabbed for us.

No way to fight them off. All three of us were dragged from the van.

Luke tried to kick his way free. He swung both fists. But two other Horrors moved quickly to hold Luke down.

Clay uttered a terrified moan and shook his head sadly as the Horrors led us away.

I turned back — and saw a Horror handing a thick green stack of something to Derek and Margo. Money?

Yes.

The Horrors were paying the Stranges.

The Stranges had been working for them all along.

"Why?" I called back to them, my voice breaking with fear. "Why did you do this to us?"

Derek ignored me. He was busy counting the money.

Margo turned, her expression cold. "You saw too much, Lizzy," she replied. "Last summer, the first time you came to HorrorLand, the three of you saw too much. And you were willing to tell the world about it."

"Wh-what do you mean?" I stammered.

"You were willing to go on TV and expose HorrorLand," Margo explained. "The Horrors can't allow that. If you had said no to Derek and me, we would have left you alone. But now . . ."

"Now *what*?" I cried.

Margo frowned. "Now you can never leave."

The Horrors started to drag us away again.

"But we won't tell anyone!" Luke called to the Stranges. "We'll keep quiet! Promise!"

"Yes. Let us go, and we won't say a word!" I cried.

"Too late," Derek said. He stuffed the wad of bills into his jacket pocket. Then he motioned to Margo. They climbed back into the van. A few seconds later, it roared away.

"Ow!" I cried out as a Horror's clawed hand tightened around my shoulder. "Where are you taking us?" I demanded shakily.

He pointed to a tall mountain, rising darkly at the back of the park. "We're taking you to a new attraction up at the top," he rasped. "It's called the Final Leap."

"And . . . what are we going to do there?" I asked.

"Three guesses," he replied.

struggled to think clearly. But my panic made my brain whir.

Everything seemed to be speeded up, as if we were all moving in fast-forward. The Horrors, the park, Luke and Clay — they were all a blur to me. Sights and sounds that didn't add up to anything, that didn't make sense.

I kept taking deep breaths and holding them, trying to slow my pounding heart, trying to focus my eyes, focus my thoughts.

I kept watching for a chance to escape. I saw that Luke and Clay were tensed, also watching for their chance.

But a dozen Horrors guarded us closely. No way to break away. No way to run.

They shoved us into a little monorail train car. It

was tiny — room for five or six at the most. But the Horrors all jammed in with us.

The car creaked and groaned as it twisted and curved up the steep mountain. At one point, it jerked hard, and we were all crushed against one wall of the car.

"Please, let us out," I tried begging one more time. "We promise we won't tell anyone about HorrorLand. We'll sign a paper. We'll do whatever you want."

The Horrors ignored me.

The little train car jerked to a hard stop. The doors slid open. They shoved us out.

"Whoa." I uttered a frightened cry as I gazed around.

We stood on a narrow cliff that jutted out from the mountainside. And down below . . . down below . . .

I shut my eyes. I shouldn't have looked down.

It had to be a mile drop, straight down. And at the bottom, I saw dark, jagged rocks, sharp points reaching up like spikes.

"Welcome to the Final Leap," a Horror said cheerfully. "This is our most thrilling attraction. It's the most exciting free-fall ride in the world. The sad thing is, it lasts only a few seconds."

"Oh, please . . .," Luke whispered. He had his eyes shut tight. He grabbed my hand.

"You . . . you're not really going to make us

jump — are you?" Clay asked in a whisper. All the color had faded from his face. I could see his legs trembling.

"Take your time," a Horror replied.

"Shut your eyes. It makes it easier," another Horror chimed in.

"Maybe you should hold hands and all jump at once," the first Horror said.

"Scream your heads off," another Horror added. "Don't worry about it. We're far away from everyone else. No one will hear you."

The Horrors backed up, leaving us on the edge of the cliff. I gazed down again at the jagged, dark rocks so far below.

I swallowed hard. My mouth felt as dry as cotton.

"We won't do it," I told them. "You can wait all day. We won't jump."

"No problem," a Horror replied. The others stepped out of the way as he moved to a bright yellow lever that jutted out from a metal control panel.

He grabbed the lever with both hands and shoved it down.

I heard a rumbling sound.

The cliff trembled beneath our feet.

And then it started to slide — slide into the mountainside.

It's going to slide out from under us, I realized.

We aren't going to survive. We really are going to fall.

I grabbed the boys' hands and held on tightly.

Below us, the cliff floor slid rapidly. We had no room . . . nowhere to stand . . .

"Sorry . . . ," I whispered. "Good-bye, Luke. Good-bye, Clay. Good-bye."

I held on tightly to the boys' hands. And shut my eyes.

The cliff rumbled and slid . . . slid . . .

Only a few feet of cliff floor left.

The wind whipped around us.

My legs started to give away.

I held my breath. Prepared to fall.

I heard voices behind me.

I turned in time to see a Horror push the yellow lever back up.

The cliff floor rumbled to a stop.

The three of us stood right on the edge. The front of my shoes hung over the side.

Three new Horrors had joined the others. "You are wanted down below," one of the new ones said. "Leave the prisoners to us."

The first group of Horrors nodded. They jammed

into the monorail car and a few seconds later rumbled away.

Out on the narrow cliff, I didn't have room to turn around. But I glanced over my shoulder at the new group of Horrors. "Are you rescuing us?" I called. "We don't have to jump?"

The Horror leader narrowed his yellow eyes at us. "We have our own plans for you," he growled.

The three Horrors stepped forward. They grabbed us and tugged us off the narrow cliff ledge.

"Let's go. Quickly," the leader growled.

We made our way, lurching and stumbling, down the steep mountain, following the curve of the monorail tracks.

"What are you going to do to us?" Luke demanded. "Where are you taking us?"

"Don't speak," the Horror rasped. He gave Luke a hard shove in the back.

The sun had set. A gray mist had settled over the park. The air felt cold and damp.

I shivered.

At the bottom of the mountain, the Horrors forced us along a hidden pathway. It led to a tall fence at the back of the park. A sign over a narrow opening read: EMPLOYEES ONLY. NO EXIT.

"Hurry," the Horror ordered.

They shoved us through the narrow opening. We stumbled into a dark, empty lot. A black van was parked near the fence, the motor running.

"Where are you taking us?" I cried. "We won't tell anyone anything. We swear!"

"Quiet!" the leader barked.

They slid open the side door and forced us inside. We squeezed onto the backseat. They slammed the door shut and climbed in the front.

"Please —" I begged. "Please —"

The three Horrors pulled off their masks. Two young men and a blond-haired woman smiled at us. "You're okay now," the woman said. "You're safe."

"You — you're *rescuing* us?" I cried.

They nodded.

"Those Horrors are real monsters," the man behind the wheel said solemnly. "They're evil creatures. They've built this whole park to torture humans."

"Why?" I asked.

"Torturing humans is a sport to them. In fact, it's their most popular sport," he replied. "But thanks to you three, they will be exposed. The Stranges have been arrested. And HorrorLand will be shut down forever."

"But — who are you?" I demanded.

"We're from a TV show," the woman replied, brushing back her hair. "Maybe you've seen it. It's called *Weird Copy*. We report on all the weird things going on in the world."

"We've been watching you kids the whole time," the man added. "We got it all on film. This is going to make a terrific TV show."

He turned to the front and put the van in gear. We roared off down the road.

"Thank you!" Luke cried happily. "Thank you for saving us!"

"Are you going to take us home now?" Clay asked eagerly.

"Well . . . we've got one more stop," the woman replied.

"Huh? One more stop?" I asked.

She nodded. "The story isn't quite finished. We need to add a few more exciting moments."

"Whoa," I murmured. "Exciting moments? What do you mean?"

"You'll see . . . ," she replied, turning her face to the window.

We rode in silence. A short while later, the van pulled into a big, crowded parking lot.

And I let out a scream as I stared up at a huge blue-and-green neon sign:

WELCOME TO TERRORVILLE.

About R.L. Stine

R.L. Stine is the most popular author in America. He is the creator of the *Goosebumps, Give Yourself Goosebumps, Fear Street*, and *Ghosts of Fear Street* series, among other popular books. He has written over 250 scary novels for kids. Bob lives in New York City with his wife, Jane, teenage son, Matt, and dog, Nadine.

Welcome to the new millennium of fear

Check out this
chilling preview of
what's next from
R.L. STINE

Jekyll and Heidi

"**Y**our uncle's name is Jekyll, right?" Aaron asked softly. "Maybe he's a great-great-grandson of the original Dr. Jekyll. Maybe —"

"But that's just a *story*!" I cried. "Do you know the difference, Aaron? There's *fiction* — and there's *nonfiction*. Dr. Jekyll is *fiction*."

"But the monster is *real*," he insisted. "Everyone in the whole county is afraid to go out at night. We only have four police officers in the village. They don't know what to do."

"They should stop watching scary movies at night," I joked. "Then they wouldn't have these nightmares."

"Fine. Okay," Aaron snapped angrily. "Don't believe me. Make jokes. But you should know this, Heidi. The villagers want your uncle arrested.

The police just haven't been able to find enough proof."

"How do you know so much about the police?" I demanded.

"My cousin Allan is on the force," he replied. "Besides, it's a small village. Everyone knows everything around here. Even the kids."

I stared hard at him, studying his face. He seemed sincere with this monster story. But of course it was a joke. It had to be.

I shivered. "I've got to get to Uncle Jekyll's." I sighed. "Is there a taxi?"

He shook his head. "You can walk there. It's only about twenty minutes or so from here."

"Point me in the right direction," I said.

He pointed to the road. "Just follow it. Your uncle's house is at the top of the hill."

I squinted at the trees, heavy with snow. "Does the house have a street number?"

"No," Aaron replied. "But you can't miss it. It's a huge mansion. It looks like an evil castle in an old horror movie. Really."

"Yes, I kind of remember it," I said. Then I had an idea. "Can you walk me there? Can you come with me?"

Aaron lowered his eyes to the ground. "I . . . can't," he murmured. He grabbed my arm. "Please, Heidi. You understand, right? I don't want to die."

I knew Aaron was kidding me. I knew his whole story had to be some kind of joke. But why did I see so much fear in his eyes? Was he just a good actor?

"Well, maybe I'll see you around," I said. "You know. In town. Or in school."

"Yeah. Catch you later." He turned and ran toward the bus station. He glanced back at me once, then disappeared around the back.

He's probably hurrying to tell his mom about the joke he played on the new girl in town, I decided. The two of them are probably laughing their heads off now.

I took a deep breath, tightened my parka hood over my head, and started walking. The hard-packed snow crunched under my Doc Martens.

Glittering snow-drops fell from the trees, silvery in the late afternoon sun.

"What a horrible day," I murmured. First, Uncle Jekyll doesn't show. Then I meet a kid who just wants to terrify me with a stupid joke about how my uncle is a monster. Then I have to walk all the way to his house in the freezing cold.

The narrow road sloped up a low hill through the village. I studied the small shops. A barber-shop with a snow-covered barber pole, a general store, a tiny post office with a fluttering flag over the door, a gun store with a display of hunting rifles filling the window.

This is it, I realized. The whole village. Just two blocks long.

A snowy side street curving up from the main road had rows of little houses on each side. They looked like tiny boxes, one after another.

I wondered if Aaron lived in one of those houses.

I leaned into the gusting wind and followed the road up the hill. As I left town, the woods began again. The tree branches creaked and groaned, shifting in the breeze. I heard small animals scuttling over the ground. Squirrels, I thought. Or maybe raccoons.

The road curved sharply. I still hadn't passed a single person or car. My backpack bounced on my shoulders as I climbed.

"Oh." I uttered a sharp cry as Uncle Jekyll's

house suddenly came into view. The house — it *did* look like an evil castle from an old horror movie.

Wet snow-drops from the trees blew into my eyes, blurring my vision. I wiped the snow away and stared up at the enormous dark stone mansion.

My new home.

A sob escaped my throat. I quickly swallowed it.

You're going to be fine, Heidi, I told myself. Don't start feeling sorry for yourself before you even give it a chance.

"It's an adventure," I murmured out loud.

Yes. I planned to think of my new life as an adventure.

My eyes on the house, I trudged up the steep hill. My shoes slipped in the wet snow. The wind swirled around me, roaring louder as I approached the top.

A few minutes later, I stepped into the shadow of the house. The sun seemed to disappear. I blinked in the blue-gray darkness.

And made my way onto the stone steps that led to the black wooden door. I pushed the doorbell.

Why was I shaking all over? From the cold?

I brushed wet snow-drops from the front of my parka and pushed the doorbell again.

And waited. Waited. Trembling. Breathing hard.

Finally, the heavy door creaked open.

A head poked out. A pretty girl's face ringed by long black curls.

Marianna!

"Hi —" I started.

But I didn't get another word out.

"Get away from here!" she whispered furiously. *"Get away while you can!"*

5

"**H**uh?" I gasped and nearly fell off the stone steps. "Marianna — what do you mean?"

Her dark eyes flashed. She opened her mouth to reply.

But she suddenly stopped.

I heard the click of footsteps approaching on the hardwood floor. Marianna turned back to the house.

A maid in a black uniform and white apron appeared. "It's my cousin Heidi," Marianna explained to the young woman.

The maid laughed. "Well, Marianna, aren't you going to let her in?"

Marianna narrowed her eyes at me, as if warning me again. Then her face went blank, no expression at all. She pulled open the heavy door and motioned for me to enter.

"This is Sylvia," Marianna said, pointing to the maid. "She will help you unpack."

"Your bags arrived two days ago," Sylvia said. "Did you walk from the station?"

I nodded. I still had my parka hood up. I tugged it down and started to unzip my coat.

"I reminded Dad this morning that you were coming," Marianna said, shaking her head. "He probably forgot."

"You must be frozen," Sylvia said, taking my coat. "I'll make something hot to drink." She hurried away, her shoes clicking on the floor.

I glanced around. Marianna and I stood in a dark entryway. High overhead, a large glass chandelier cast pale light that hardly seemed to reach the floor. The walls were papered dark green. The aroma of roasting meat filled the room.

I turned to Marianna. She was tall, at least six inches taller than me, and thin. Her black curls flowed down behind a heavy red-and-white plaid ski sweater. She wore black leggings that made her look even taller.

Again — seven years later — I felt pale and colorless standing next to her.

She crossed her arms over the front of her sweater and led me into a large living room. A fire blazed in a stone fireplace at one end. Heavy brown leather furniture faced the fireplace.

Enormous paintings of snowy-peaked mountain landscapes covered one wall. The curtains were pulled halfway over the front window, allowing in only a narrow rectangle of light.

"How *are* you?" I asked my cousin, forcing some enthusiasm.

"Okay," she replied flatly.

"Are you on winter break?" I asked.

She nodded. "Yeah." Her arms were still crossed tightly in front of her.

"How is Uncle Jekyll?" I tried.

"Okay, I guess," she replied, shrugging. "Real busy."

Marianna is as shy as ever, I decided.

But then I asked myself: Is she shy — or unfriendly?

I kept trying to start a conversation. "Where *is* Uncle Jekyll? Is he home?"

"He's working," Marianna replied, moving to the window. "In his lab. He can't be disturbed." She turned her back to me and stared out at the snow.

"Well . . . shouldn't I tell him I'm here?" I asked. I picked up a small blue glass bird. Some kind of hawk. I needed something to do with my hands. The glass bird was surprisingly heavy. I set it back down.

Marianna didn't answer my question.

"I walked through the village," I said. "It's pretty tiny. What do you do for fun? Where do you hang out? I mean . . . there *are* other kids our age, right?"

She nodded, but didn't reply. The gray light flooding in from the window made her look like a beautiful statue.

When she finally uncrossed her arms and turned to me, she had the coldest expression on her face. Cold as stone.

"Want to see your room?" she asked.

"Yes. Definitely!" I replied. I followed her to the front stairway. I slid one hand over the smooth black banister as we made the steep climb.

Marianna is just very shy, I decided. She must feel so weird, having a total stranger, someone her own age, move in with her.

"I — I hope we can be like sisters," I blurted out.

A strange, snickering laugh escaped her lips. She stopped on the stairs and turned back to me. "Sisters?"

"Well . . . yeah," I replied, my heart suddenly pounding. "I know this must be kind of hard for you. I mean —"

She sneered. "Kind of hard? You don't know *anything*, Heidi."

"What do you mean?" I demanded. "Tell me."

She swept her black curls back over her shoulders and continued climbing. We reached the second floor.

I stared up and down an endless hallway of darkly flowered wallpaper. The air felt cold and damp. Lights on torch-shaped wall sconces cast a pale glow down the hall. Most of the doors were closed.

"That's my room there," Marianna said, pointing. It appeared to be a mile away at the end of the hall. She pushed open a heavy door. "And this is your room."

I shut my eyes as I stepped inside. I knew it was going to be gross. Dark and depressing.

When I opened my eyes, I smiled in surprise. "Not bad," I murmured.

The room was totally cheerful. Afternoon sunlight poured in through airy, light curtains on two large windows. I quickly took in a single bed with my suitcases opened on it, a little wooden desk, a tall dresser, two modern-looking chairs.

Not bad at all.

One wall had floor-to-ceiling bookshelves jammed with books.

Marianna stood in the doorway watching me. "You'll probably want to take Dad's old books out and put your own stuff on the shelves," she said.

"No. I like books," I replied. "Did my computer arrive? And my CD player?"

"Not yet," Marianna replied.

I moved to the window, pushed the curtains aside, and peered out. "What a great view!" I exclaimed. "I can see all the way down the hill to the village!"

"Thrills," Marianna muttered.

I turned to face her. "Are you in a bad mood or something?"

She shrugged. "Sylvia will help you unpack your suitcases, if you want."

"No. I want to do it myself," I replied. I walked to a door next to the dresser. "Is this the closet?"

I didn't wait for her to answer. I pulled open the door and stared into an endlessly long closet with shelves and poles on both sides.

"Wow!" I exclaimed. "This is awesome! This closet is almost as big as my whole room back home!"

Back home . . .

The words caught in my throat. I was surprised by the wave of emotion that swept over me.

Tears brimmed in my eyes, and I quickly wiped them away.

I leaned into the closet so Marianna wouldn't see me cry. Get over it, Heidi, I scolded myself. *This* is your home now.

But I wasn't over it.

I wasn't over the tragedy that had changed my life, that had brought me to this strange house in this tiny New England village.

I'll *never* get over it, I thought bitterly, picturing my parents' smiling faces.

I took a couple of deep breaths. Then I stepped out of the closet. "Marianna, this closet is really —"

She wasn't there. She had vanished.

"What is her *problem*?" I asked out loud.

I moved to the bed and started pulling T-shirts and tops from the first suitcase. I carried them to the dresser and began piling them in a drawer. The dresser smelled a little mildewy. I hoped my clothes wouldn't pick up the smell.

I filled up the first drawer, then stopped. I really should say hi to Uncle Jekyll, I decided. I really should let him know that I've arrived.

Tugging down the sleeves of my sweater, I hurried out into the hall and made my way to the steps. My heart started to pound. I hadn't seen Uncle Jekyll since I was five.

Would he be happy to see me? I hope he gives me a warmer welcome than Marianna, I thought nervously.

"Heidi — where are you going?"

I turned at the sound of Marianna's voice from down the hall. She poked her head out of her room.

"Down to say hi to Uncle Jekyll," I told her.

"He's in his lab. You really shouldn't disturb him," she called.

"I'll just say hi and then hurry out," I replied.

I ran into Sylvia at the bottom of the stairs. She pointed me in the direction of my uncle's lab.

Down another long hallway. I stopped in front of the lab door.

I raised my hand to knock. But a loud noise on the other side of the door made me jerk my hand back.

It sounded like an animal grunt. A pig, maybe.

I held my breath and listened.

Another pig grunt. Followed by frightening cries. Like an animal caught in a trap. An animal in pain.

I couldn't stand it any longer.

I pushed open the door.

My uncle stood hunched over a long table with his back to me. His long white lab coat came down nearly to the floor.

He dipped his head. And I heard another squeal. Not a human cry. An animal cry.

It's true! I thought, frozen in terror.

He really is acting out the old Jekyll-Hyde story.

Uncle Jekyll drank some weird chemicals. And he turned himself into a terrifying creature!

And then as I stared at him from the doorway, he turned.

Slowly, he turned to face me.

And I uttered a horrified gasp.

PREPARE TO BE SCARED!

Goosebumps®
SERIES 2000
R.L. STINE